SEA OF CRYSTAL,
SEA OF GLASS

SEA OF CRYSTAL, SEA OF GLASS

BENITA J. PRINS

ISBN 978-1988615189

Previously published as *Seascape*.

Cover & interior design by Benita J. Prins
Kairos Book Design & Editing |
kairosbookdesign.com

First paperback printing, May 2016
Third edition, May 2021

TO ELIZABETH & THERESA

"Greater love than this has no man,
that he lay down his life for his friends."
John 15:13

TABLE OF CONTENTS

1

BE NOT AFRAID

One moment the skies were clear; the next, rain fled from them in terrified haste. Einur raced for his cave shelter, leaving his sheep, undisturbed by the downpour, still ripping up grass. Reaching the cave, he crouched just inside, shivering – already drenched despite his swift retreat from the open field.

As his shivers subsided, he raised his fingers to his mouth and blew a shrill whistle. Presently there came the beat of wings, and a dark form alighted beyond the cave opening.

"Come here, Efrix," commanded Einur, and the dragon slithered in. His body fit snugly within the stone walls; he was a small specimen of his kind.

"Einur?" came a second voice from outside.

"Is that you, Gernhr?"

"Einur!" Gernhr's voice was filled with terror. "You must come at once!"

Einur's heart nearly stopped.

Lody.

"Move!" he snapped at Efrix, shoving at the dragon's scaly side with his hands. Slowly the creature wedged himself back out, Einur impatient with fear behind him.

"Have they taken Lody?" he shouted, taking hold of Gernhr's shoulders and shaking his friend. "Where is she?"

Gernhr broke free and shook his head, trying to catch his breath. "No, no, Einur, not Lody. Einur, *your* name was drawn!"

Einur's mind froze in relief at Gernhr's initial reassurance, the latter part of his statement not registering at once. Then it filtered through.

"*My* name?"

The thought of this happening had never once occurred to the boy. Rather, the possibility which had haunted him ever since his little sister's birth was that she would be chosen, that she would be taken to the Temple from where no child had ever returned. That Lody would be sacrificed to the

Great Achiel.

Not me.

Gernhr was watching him when the dizzy blackness faded from his vision. "You know what we planned if Lody was chosen, Einur. It's little different now it's you instead of her. You can run off, Einur, live in the wild somewhere. I'll even come with you, if you want me to."

He broke off and stared at Einur, whose eyes were glassy and confused.

"You aren't going with the Illyrië, are you?"

Einur revived himself. "I'll leave right now. But you mustn't come with me; your dad needs you. Your ma will take care of Lody, no?"

Gernhr nodded. Then he tensed.

"They're coming!"

Einur stood still for three seconds, but he did not have Gernhr's swift hearing.

"Run! They've tracked you here!"

"Efrix!" called Einur, and quickly embraced his friend. "Goodbye, Gernhr. Tell Lody I love her, and I'll come back as soon as I can."

He jumped onto Efrix's back and exclaimed, "Go!"

The dragon didn't move. Einur repeated his order once, twice, panic leaping into his voice.

"What are you doing, Einur? Go!" shouted Gernhr.

Einur glanced behind him; the hirelings of the Illyrië were in sight now, coming over a small hillock. There were ten or so, perhaps fifteen. Einur kicked Efrix hard in the sides.

"Go, you stupid creature!"

Still Efrix remained on the ground.

"Just leave him and run!"

The pursuers were only a few hundred feet away. Einur gave them one look and slipped off Efrix's back, running now for dear life up into the bracken. His path led him up the side of a small mountain, yet his pace slowed not at all. The yells of his enemies were close behind him – with every step he took, he expected to be yanked back. Gradually, however, the shouts grew further away, and then died out altogether. Einur allowed himself one brief pause and looked down the mountainside. His would-be captors had become worn out by the race up the steep slope, and had retreated. He couldn't see Gernhr anymore; please the Great Achiel he was unharmed.

But won't the Great Achiel be enraged that he helped the sacrifice escape? he thought. Yet he could do nothing but turn and go on.

His steps soon became stumbling, and presently rest was imperative. If only Efrix hadn't been so stubborn, Einur could've ridden on him instead. But what a ridiculous thing for the dragon to suddenly do! Why, everyone used dragons as their mounts; the creatures were bred for that very purpose!

The dragon himself landed beside Einur just then.

"You wicked creature!" the boy told it, and it snorted and nuzzled its snout up against his shoulder. He gave it a slap and repeated his admonishment, but the slap was gentle and the rebuke no harsher.

They settled into positions as comfortable as the rain-soaked ground and Einur's wet clothes allowed. Einur still made a pretence of being angry; but Efrix let out periodic soft snorts until his master rubbed the top of his scaly head and laughed, "You ought to be ashamed of yourself!"

They went to sleep with Einur snuggled against Efrix's warm side.

Einur woke early to find Efrix again gone but the sun returned. As he waited for Efrix to come back

– as he was sure the dragon would – he breakfasted off henla, a type of leaf that grew year-round and was very nourishing. The flavour was slightly tart, making the leaves an invigorating morning meal. He was finishing his breakfast when Efrix arrived.

"Where did you go?" he asked, rubbing his hand up and down Efrix's back. "Have you found breakfast? Good, let's go!"

He climbed onto Efrix and the dragon lifted off. The day was beautiful; there wasn't a cloud anywhere in the azure sky, and a light breeze blew Einur's blond hair off his shoulders.

The sun showed it was little past noon when they alighted to find some sort of dinner. Einur found nothing but more henla leaves; he ate these whilst Efrix flew off to look for his own dinner.

He woke from a brief nap feeling delightfully warm and extremely relaxed. Through his still-closed eyelids the sunlight streamed into his mind, and he drank it in lazily. Then something blocked the light, and irritably he opened his eyes to see what had happened.

Over him, staring down into his face, stood a man, his hair and beard pale green, and his eyes sea-blue. He wore forest-green robes and carried a long staff engraved with the recurring motif of a fish.

"Einur, is it not?"

Einur scrambled onto his feet. "How do you know my name?"

"I have my sources," replied the man. "And as I do know it, in fairness I should give you mine. I am Eigion, and some of what I know, you must learn."

"Learn what?"

"What you must know to perform your task."

Without realising it, Einur was backing away from the stranger ever so gradually. "What task?"

"Stop moving!" commanded Eigion, and abruptly Einur noticed his slight movements backward and stopped. "Sit, and I will explain everything to you."

Einur sat in obedience, and Eigion seated himself facing the boy. He laid his staff on the ground beside him and drummed on his cheek with long fingers, his eyes keenly taking in everything observable about Einur. Einur flushed and scowled.

"I haven't got all the time in the world. If you have something to tell me, you had better do it quickly."

A smile darted across Eigion's lips. "You should do well," he said cryptically. "Are you a follower of the cult of the Great Achiel?"

"Of course," muttered Einur, but the hatred in his eyes gave the lie to his words.

"Despite your attempt to conceal it, you hate the cult and all that goes with it. Do you not?"

Einur's glance jumped up to meet Eigion's, then descended again to the ground. He did not reply.

"Do you not?"

Einur was still silent, but Eigion did not look away from him.

"Do you need me to answer?" Einur said at last.

"I know what your answer is, yes, but I do need you to tell me yourself."

"Why?"

"Why do you not wish to answer me?"

"Oh, all right. Yes, I hate the Great Achiel, and I hate the Illyrië, and the whole business. Now you can execute me. That's what you want, after all."

Eigion smiled, a genuine smile. "That was the thing furthest from my mind."

"What was closer, then?" Einur was still argumentative in his tones, but he could not deny to himself that he was interested in this man – or whatever he was – greatly interested. He wanted to know of what task Eigion spoke, and against his wishes he began to believe that Eigion was probably on his side... *Side? Where did that idea come from?*

"Although you hate it, do you believe in its truth?"

It was a question Einur had never considered in his sixteen years, and it gave him pause. Finally he answered, "Yes."

"Why?"

He was honest. "I've no idea."

"Give it up."

Einur might have hated the cult and wished to leave it, but still he was shocked at the blunt words that suggested such a thing. "*Give it up?*"

"So I said."

"But why?"

"So many questions! Not only have you no conviction in your belief, but had you, it were wrongly placed. There is truth in the cult of Achiel only in the sense that there is at least a seed of truth in everything; besides this, there is only evil." He held up his hand to prevent Einur's open mouth from generating a horrified response to his disrespect of the Great Achiel's name. "No more questions, Einur Landman! Listen now, and question after. For what I have just stated is the basis of your task.

"I will begin my story far back in the history of Kelyan. Precisely five thousand years after the creation of the world, the Second Tribe of Lo'Rien rebelled against the Master of the Kelyanic Harmony, creating their own demonic cult worship, the very one to which men yet hold this very day. The First Tribe also succumbed to the evil spread by the Second Tribe, but the Third Tribe refused to join with the others. Battle was joined between the Tribes; the First and Second were victorious, and the remnants of the Third escaped into... well, into oblivion."

"Doesn't anyone know where they went?" exclaimed Einur before Eigion could continue.

The older man shook his head.

"Is my task to find them?" Einur was curiously intrigued by Eigion's tale, and the mystery of the lost Tribe called to him somehow.

"Partly."

Einur repressed a cheer. "What else?"

"Listen." The rebuke was impressively gentle, but it completely quenched Einur's eagerness. "Unless it is checked, the cult of the Great Achiel will continue to grow in evil, as it has for the past five thousand years. However, it cannot be checked, except by one means."

Again excitement surged from Einur's heart to his throat. "How?"

Eigion did not answer his question directly. "The first part of your task is to find the lost Third Tribe; more precisely, to find their king. That is the easy part."

Certainly Einur was excited about this quest, yet he gulped now. "That's the easy part? They've been lost for five thousand years and that's the *easy* part?"

"The second part is more vague. The fall of the cult can be caused only by a sacrifice made by one person."

"What kind of sacrifice?" Visions of the culture of human sacrifice in which he'd grown up flitted through the young man's head, and he thought of his little sister.

"That is unknown." Seeming to sense the uncertainty now tormenting Einur, he added, "But it is not of the kind of which you are thinking."

"So I'm supposed to find this tribe that's been lost practically since the beginning of time, and then someone's supposed to make a sacrifice that no one knows any details of."

"I am glad to see that you have absorbed my instructions so well."

Einur sat silently for some time. *If I do this, I supposedly have a chance of getting rid of the danger to Lody... if they don't draw her name whilst I'm gone, which is actually quite likely, considering they probably cheat at the drawing... But this quest thing is such a ridiculous idea! Yet if there's a possibility of giving Lody better chances of surviving her ninth year... What else am I going to do with myself anyway? I can't go back home now, and it can't really hurt me much to go journeying all over Kelyan. And really, I'd do anything to destroy something that might hurt Lody. Doesn't hurt that it's an evil cult either.*

"I'll go."

Eigion nodded. "Do you trust me?"

"Yes."

"No, Einur. Do you trust me?"

Confused, Einur repeated his answer.

"Einur! It is not enough to *say* you trust me. You must *trust* me. Think about it first, as you did about accepting your task. I do not wish you to take this lightly. You *must not* take this lightly."

Again Einur sat in thought. Yes, he trusted Eigion – to a human degree at least. True, the man was unlike anyone he'd ever met, but this somehow didn't decrease his trust, instead increasing it; few of the people in Einur's life had been worthy of trust, and the differences between the Illyrië and Eigion attracted him. Besides this, there was also an aura about Eigion which spoke of something much greater than the man.

He was about to tell Eigion this when Efrix returned, alighting close beside his master. The dragon observed Eigion with as much suspicion as a dumb creature can gather. Efrix seemed to shrink from the stranger, and if dragons had had the capacity to fear man, Einur would have said that without a doubt, his dragon was terrified of Eigion.

Eigion was frowning. "That is your dragon, if I am not mistaken."

Einur nodded briefly, but changed the subject back to the previous one. "I do trust you, sir, with all my heart."

"Are you willing to prove it?"

Confused, Einur blinked. "Yes?" he almost questioned.

Eigion unbuckled something from around his waist and held it out to Einur: a long sword in a plain leather scabbard.

"Take it."

Einur took it, his stomach suddenly alive with nervousness.

"Now kill the dragon."

He nearly dropped the sword. "Kill *Efrix*?"

Eigion only stared at him.

"But he's my mount, he's my friend!"

"On your quest against evil, no dragon is a friend of yours. Did you not say that you trust me?"

Slowly, Einur turned to Efrix. Efrix – yes, it was Efrix, but at the same time it was not Efrix. The dragon's coal-black eyes were turning red, and its chest blazed orange: the latter a clear sign of anger, the former a phenomenon Einur had never seen in a dragon.

Then Efrix spoke.

"If you kill me, you too will find death."

Einur shrieked aloud.

"If you kill me, you will find despair."

Einur continued to scream.

"If you kill me, you will find oblivion."

"Enough!"

It was Eigion's voice, but deeper and richer than before, and it quieted the dragon for a moment. Efrix turned his eyes to Eigion, and seemed no longer afraid of the man but contemptuous.

"And as for you, you fool..."

"Enough, foul creature!" Eigion cried again. "Einur, kill him now!"

Trembling uncontrollably, Einur stooped and raised the sword, which he had dropped when

Efrix first spoke. The fingers of his right hand wrapped convulsively around the hilts, he faced what had been his dragon – and now seemed to be so once more. Efrix's eyes were again a normal black, and his chest silver-grey like the rest of his scales. Despite what Einur had just witnessed, a doubt filled his mind. Had it not been but a dream?

Did you not say that you trust me?

He looked towards Eigion, who now did or said nothing to influence the young man's decision. He looked back at Efrix, who gazed at him with his familiar, submissive, friendly gaze.

Did you not say that you trust me?

A sudden conviction filled Einur, a conviction that by distrusting Eigion, he distrusted something – or someone – far greater. He raised the sword... and drove it with all his might into Efrix's neck.

2

IF YOU FOLLOW ME

How am I to travel without Efrix?"

That was the question Einur had asked Eigion before they parted two days ago... and now here he was, exhaustedly pulling himself through the doghole on the north end of his family's longhouse. Once inside, he collapsed onto the ground and lay curled into an inert ball, too tired even to wiggle a toe. *Must say farewell to Lody* bounced back and forth in his mind - and then he fell asleep.

He was alone in the longhouse: he and his sister lived by themselves. Over five years ago their parents had left on a trip round the Circled Hills to Mourvh, the nearest village, but they'd never reached it. A week after their departure, a farmer from the area of the Thema Pass brought the news that the couple had been captured by the savages of the Pass - savages notorious for their merciless cruelty. Rendered a suspicious child by his mother's pronounced favouritism of his sister over himself, the nearly ten-year-old Einur had refused all aid from neighbours, electing to raise Aloden, almost seven years younger, alone.

In the late afternoon he was awoken by a soft kiss on his cheek. The same thought - *Must say farewell to Lody* - popped back into his head as he woke; and, opening his eyes, he found that Lody herself was leaning over him.

"Why'd you go away without giving me good-bye?" she chirped. "But I guess you're back. Let's go tell Gernhr you're back."

Einur sat up and shook his head violently, sending his hair flying into a mess. "You mustn't tell anyone I'm here, Lody!" he whispered. "I'm hiding."

"From the Illyrië? Gernhr said they were after you. Is't so? Why'd you come back if it's so?"

"I had to give you good-bye," he replied, echoing

her own words. "I couldn't go away forever without giving you good-bye."

She dropped into his lap and flung her little arms around his neck. "Will you take me with you, Einur? Please take me with you, please? I don't want to stay here without you."

He detached himself gently from her grasp. "I'm sorry, Lody - I'm afraid I can't." A plump tear and trembling lips threatened a storm; he hastily continued. "You'll be safe with Gernhr's ma. She'll take care of you ever so much better than I can."

"No, I won't be safe!" The storm began, relatively calm at first but gaining intensity. "They'll pick me, Einur, they'll pick me, I promise you!"

Einur stared at the eight-year-old, startled by the certainty in her tone. It wasn't simply the tantrum of an affectionate little girl afraid of losing her brother; she sounded absolutely sure. This so disquieted him that he was unable to find words to reassure her.

"Don't say they won't, Einur, 'cause they will. Please, please, please take me with you! I don't want to stay here with Auntie Lyný, she plaits my hair too tight, and I know they'll pick me!"

Einur dropped his head into his hands and

drove the tips of his fingers into his temples. How in Kelyan was he to get out of this? He was adamant he wouldn't take his baby sister away into the wild, yet it seemed – no, it was too unkind to leave her here when she was so frightened. Could he wait till she fell asleep that night and then...

Voices. Still a little distant, but not far enough, and coming closer: angry and loud voices; voices he feared... He froze, feeling like an ice statue as a horrible chilled feeling seeped from his heart throughout his entire body.

"Lody, get out of here now!" he hissed.

For a moment he thought she was going to ask why, but she closed her mouth and skittered through the doghole. Outside, she turned around and peeped back in at her brother, eyes wide.

"Get away!"

She scooted.

He could hear them fiddling with the latch of the door on the other side of the longhouse; his heart grew colder yet and he flung himself towards the doghole. He shoved his head through it, then began to wrestle his shoulders after his head. The hole had been cut for a tall but lean dog, not for a well-grown boy. They'd be inside any second now.

He closed his eyes and wriggled, tadpole fashion.

"Here he is!"

Einur's eyes flew open, and he stared up into a craggy face. He knew the man; he'd worked for Einur's father a couple times – years back, but Einur had never forgotten his harshness, the crude language he'd used, or his nastiness to all those over whom he was superior. What was his name again?

"Out you come, boy." Galaser took hold of Einur under the shoulders and gave several sharp yanks. The method worked admirably; Einur popped out like a cork under a good deal of pressure. "Why'd you run, kid? Don't you want to do your duty to the Great Achiel, hey?"

Einur gave a sudden, vicious kick backward, wrenched himself out of the man's grip, and took off. As he came past the corner of the longhouse, however, another figure jumped onto him, knocking him flat.

"Thought you'd get away, did you?" Galaser added a few of the offensive words Einur remembered, and returned the young man's kick. He and the other fellow rolled their captive onto his back and pulled him up by the arms in none too kindly a fashion. They paraded him around to the front of the building, where they were met by one of the Illyrië themselves, who spat at him and ordered the prisoner's hands to be tied. This was done, and Einur was led towards the east, towards the Temple.

He was completely on his own. The Ledmians stayed indoors, refusing as always to watch when sacrifices were rounded up and marched through the village. He looked for Lody but did not see her, for which he was thankful but hurt at the same time. *Where had she gotten to*, he wondered. Please the Great Ach – *no, please the Master of the Harmony*, he corrected the automatic prayer of habit – she was safe at 'Auntie' Lyný's by now. He let his eyes flit towards the blacksmith's, where Gernhr's father would be working. Was Gernhr there too? No, not a human figure in sight besides the rough men who hustled him along... but wait, a hand reached round the door of the smithy and waved slightly. Einur let out his breath and looked ahead again, not wishing to betray his friend's acknowledgement to the Illyrië.

Not a man of them spoke, and thanks to their bare feet there was nary a sound as they marched their prisoner up the road to the Temple. Einur was hustled through a small door around the side of the great stone building, and into a dank dungeon-like chamber. The place reeked with a frightful odour, causing Einur to gag as he stumbled in, encouraged by a kick from behind.

The door banged loudly as it met its frame, and he heard the heavy latch fall on the other side.

Einur backed up cautiously through the dark. He had no desire to trip over whatever might be on the ground of the chamber, nor to fall into it. Feeling his way behind him, he came into contact with the back wall. He slid down it and closed his eyes. He was nodding off to sleep when he was startled by the groan of the door again enduring its opening agonies. A dirty head of hair was thrust through, followed by a face that was grimier still.

"They says I gotter take youse up to the House."

Einur, completely resigned and apathetic now, forced his weary body to stand once more, and felt his way over to the boy. Outside, he could see that his small visitor was little older than Lody herself, and looked decidedly miserable. He said nothing, however, and gave Einur only a curious, unconcerned observation.

Einur docilely followed the child up the path towards the House of the Illyrië. He could not resist admiring the building, which he'd never seen before. It was a vast deal nicer than any of the longhouses in Ledmi itself, built of chiselled stone blocks – blocks that, it was rumoured, had been imported for the direct purpose of creating a fitting abode for the self-important Illyrië. He'd never expected to be entering the place himself.

The boy led Einur up to the front door and gave the knocker a sharp rap. Then he backed off the step, explaining, "I doesn't go in here. Youse gotter wait for someone to come."

Slowly the heavy oaken door eased open, and a man poked his head round it. The child scuttered away, and with his disappearance Einur felt that the last remnant of humanity had fled. He wrenched his expression into one that pretended indifference.

"Follow, please." The man's accent was foreign, and he gave a jerky, compulsive gesture as he spoke the words.

Einur did as he was bid, slipping through the door and tiptoeing after the man through the massive lobby. The pillars, made of a material he did not recognize, shot up into the furthest recesses of the ceiling, where their tops were hidden in obscurity. Vague noises issued through closed doors on either side; voices and occasional small crashes as through something had fallen and broken.

He shuddered, partially from the chill. There was a draft coming from somewhere unknown; the cold stone of the building made it seem colder yet.

His companion glanced back at him, inclining his head just a little. "You will be warmer soon."

At the end of the lobby, a stairwell rose majestically, and up this Einur was led. They went a short ways down the following passageway, then the man turned aside and knocked on a door to Einur's left.

"Enter."

The man pushed the door open and stood aside for Einur to precede him. The chamber in which he found himself was bare, yet despite the stone walls it was not cold. Looking to his right he saw why this was so: a great fire snarled on the hearth in the outside wall. Inexplicably Einur felt a cold sweat envelop him in its uncertain terror.

A figure rose from a chair a yard or two from the hearth, and stared at Einur for a moment or two. Then he spoke to Einur's escort.

"This is he, Lukil?"

Lukil nodded assent.

"Come here, boy."

Mechanically Einur obeyed, approaching the stranger with caution.

"What is your name?"

"Einur."

"Give me your hand, Einur." As he spoke the man reached out and took it, not waiting for Einur to follow the order. He drew Einur towards himself, towards the fire. "Sit."

Einur sat, in the chair which the man had

vacated. After a moment of silence he realised he was staring deep into the man's eyes. He made an effort to break his gaze away but found he could not. He felt himself growing dizzy, and struggled once more to look away.

His last memory was of the stranger's eyes, black as a moonless night, and hard, so hard – as hard as the bones of the mountains which surrounded Ledmi.

Einur came back to himself lying under soft linen and cushioned by a squashy feather mattress. He spent no little time merely revelling in such luxurious pleasure. It was when he remembered where he was that he leaped out of the bed as though he had been lying on the embers of the fire in that chamber.

A second later he imagined that he – or at least his right arm – was truly burning. He raised his arm and turned it to examine the underside of his wrist, which smarted intolerably. Branded there was a black mark: the initial letter of the name Achiel.

Sickness swelled up in Einur's throat as he

peered down at the brand, unable to think of anything else. All in one moment this nightmare became real to him: he was going to die.

3

LISTEN TO MY CRY

His eyes flicked back and forth – just as the snake's tongue flicked in and out. Along the pole it slid, always at the same speed, always inexorably nearing the end of the pole and the beginning of his arm. His fingers, splayed out along the stick, would have flexed in an attempt to catch hold of the snake and end its progress, but the ropes which tightly bound them down forbade his doing so.

The snake reached his hand, then stopped, hovering its head over the brand mark on his wrist. The head darted down, Einur experienced a brief pinching sensation – and then there was nothing.

A second time that day Einur woke to find himself seemingly on fire. Moaning, he dragged his eyelids upwards; his eyes uncrossed and he looked up into a dimly lit chamber. To his right was a wall; to his left was an open space in which he could hear human movements.

He tried to turn his head, but the fire burned more cruelly on his neck. Instead he managed to murmur, "Where... am... I...?"

There was a quick flurry, and a face bent down over his, blocking out the light of the one candle.

"You are awake!"

It was a woman's voice, soft yet eager, excited but with a broken note somewhere in its depths.

"Where..." Einur began to repeat himself, but the woman interrupted, laying a hand across his mouth.

"Do not try to speak. Rest. You are safe." She moved her hand to stroke his feverish forehead, and he fell asleep once more.

It was brighter now, and he could hear two people rather than one. The feeling of burning was gone, leaving him shivering a bit as if he were cold. This time he could turn his head without pain.

"Where am I?" he asked, his voice little weaker than normal.

Again that excited bustle as the woman turned to look at him. She came hurriedly to his side, followed by her companion.

"Einur – you are recovered now?"

"I'm fine, my lady," he answered. "But what is this place?"

"We're below the Temple," she told him, pushing him back as he tried to sit up. "No, keep resting. There will be action enough later."

Einur lay still for a moment, confused. "How'd I get here? The snake was biting me, that's all I remember."

The man in the background knelt down by Einur's pallet. "There hasn't been a child sacrificed to Achiel" – Einur automatically cringed at the omission of 'the Great' – "in five years. As with all the condemned children in that time, once your unconscious body was placed on the altar and was hidden by the fire's smoke, I crawled through a trapdoor in the wall and carried you down here. My wife then tended you until you regained your strength."

Another question travelled to Einur's lips and nearly escaped, when the woman shrieked softly. Her hand quaked as she pointed towards the trapdoor her husband had mentioned. Through the cracks around it seeped a greenish mist that slowly progressed towards the trio.

"Run!" shouted the man, pulling Einur up and heading for a tunnel which led westwards.

The boy stumbled after the man. He had no idea why the mist was to be feared, but he felt an instinctive revulsion for and desire to escape it. Once he glanced back to make sure the woman still followed them; she kept pace with them easily, however.

They came to a curve around which they hurtled. From ahead of Einur a splash reverberated back towards them; the woman called out, "Jump, Einur!", and he leaped into the darkness. For a couple seconds he fell freely through the air, then landed with a painful slap in icy water. He felt himself sinking and flailed frantically, desperately attempting to return to the surface. Bubbles poured from his open mouth as his last reserve of air abandoned him, and he was utterly panicked when an arm went around his middle and he came up held firmly by the man.

Even with the use of but one arm, the man's strokes were strong, and they soon reached the edge of the lake. Einur flopped onto the stone floor like a fish at the end of its death throes, lying quite still as he recovered his breath.

"Get up," commanded the man, prodding Einur with his toe. Still quivering from the lake's cold, Einur did so, and the man moved towards the most shadowy part of the wall. Following him, Einur found that what looked like a solid wall of stone actually broke apart to create the opening of a tunnel at the top of whose upward slope was a glint of light.

"Climb through this and you'll find yourself in the mountains north of Ledmi. Whatever you choose to do, stay far from the village. Not only would you be like to be recaptured, but if you were seen alive, our presence would also be revealed."

Einur nodded and squirmed his way into the slender tunnel, wriggling worm-like towards the light above him.

"The Master's blessings go with you, Einur," he heard from behind.

It was no more than five minutes before he stuck his head out and observed his surroundings. He was at the foot of a mountain, staring towards empty, dead plains. *This must be the other side of the mountains,* he thought as he took in the cheerless desert of dead grass. *Glad Ledmi's fenced in from this.*

He pulled the rest of his body out of the hole and stood up. "Where to now?" he said aloud. "Well, what did Eigion ask for? He wanted me to find the lost King. Guess here's as good a place as any to start at."

Food. He had absolutely nothing besides what he was wearing, and that was singed from the flames. *What on earth am I supposed to do?*

Go on. You said you trusted Eigion. Then do not

abandon your trust at the first sign of hardship.

Einur squared his shoulders as the words ran through his mind. He took a step forward, and another... then halted once more.

There was a little rabbit in front of him.

He frowned. *Food.* The rabbit would be food. Keeping one eye on the rabbit, he used the other to locate a sharp rock. He moved cautiously toward the creature, getting a firm hold on the rock. The rabbit didn't budge, but sat where it was, watching Einur's progress.

A foot or so from the rabbit, he crouched down. Still it didn't move. He raised the stone and began to bring it down towards the rabbit's head. Abruptly he slowed his hand. He'd seen the rabbit's eyes. They were examining him so innocently and trustingly that he couldn't kill the creature.

But I need food!

He sat motionless until he realised that the rabbit itself had to eat, and surely it would not be able to find anything in this dead wilderness. There must be some sort of food source not far away.

Einur glanced back down at the rabbit. "Go

home!" he told it.

It gave a hesitant hop towards him.

"Go on, bunny."

It turned its back on him and began to hop in the direction of the mountains. Einur followed it. They travelled a short ways, into a thicket of cedars. Even as they entered the thicket Einur could hear the giggle of a stream close by, and he felt a thirst he hadn't felt before. He saw the glitter of the water only an instant after hearing its laugh, and dove for the creek. He slurped up greedy mouthfuls of water, then turned around again. The rabbit was still there.

"Thanks."

It just stared at him.

Einur bent to pick something from the ground - a henla leaf. He sighed in ecstasy. Food. A sparse trail of the leaves led to a large patch of them, more welcome to him then than a patch of four-leafed clovers would've been. He made a good meal off them before snuggling up in the luxuriant grass.

In the morning he robbed the henla patch of most of its leaves, making a bundle of them in his tunic - the weather was summery enough that shirt and hose were sufficient.

His journey north was utterly uneventful. The infertile plains did not change into anything more lush; if there was any change at all, it was for the worse. Still, it didn't bother him. He wasn't sightseeing, he told himself, he was on a mission. The thought made him feel warm. A mission, a purpose... there hadn't been much purpose in his life thus far, besides taking care of Lody.

Lody.

He wondered what she was doing right now; perhaps crying over his supposed death. Or perhaps she'd forgotten him already. She was so little, after all. But no, he reminded himself, she wasn't that little anymore - she was nearing nine. And he'd taken care of her for five years, too; he'd been her father and mother both rolled into one. *Maybe it's best I'm gone,* he reasoned, *she needs a real mother and Gernhr's ma will love her like she deserves – maybe already does.*

He ate his midday meal on the go, stopping only for a couple minutes' rest. *Henla was certainly becoming bland and boring,* he laughed ruefully. It was practically all he'd eaten in the last few days.

Einur had barely finished his dinner when he stopped short. The lonesome feeling had disappeared, replaced with the idea that someone was behind him. He swung round but saw no one. Still, he felt a sensation that wasn't just caused by having been startled, and his heart continued beating abnormally hard. *No use in worrying though. Sure doesn't seem to be anyone in sight. And who'd be up here in the middle of nowhere at all?*

He turned his face back to the north and went on. Yet hours passed and he still felt he was being tracked. He turned around more than once but saw no signs of the supposed pursuit. All the self-reassurances he could come up with did nothing to help him fall asleep when he turned in for the night. He lay on the ground thinking he heard noises all about him.

Without warning something leapt onto him out of the dark. He gave a shriek and grabbed at it – it was a person, for he found himself clutching his attacker by the arms.

"What do you think you're up to?" he growled.

"Stop it, Einur! You're hurting me!"

The panicked voice was familiar and he let go at once. "Lody, what in Kelyan are you doing out here?"

"They're sleeping now, so I snuck away. I saw you this afternoon but they wouldn't let me call you. They made me hide whenever you looked back."

"Who?"

"The lady and man who took me away."

Anger overwhelmed Einur. How dare they pretend to be friends, saving him from the fire, and then kidnap his sister and bring her out into this wilderness!

"Show me where they are, Lody."

The child slid off Einur and took hold of his hand, leading him into the dark. A light appeared – a lantern. Einur sprang forward, loosing his sister's hand.

"Hey!"

"Is that Einur?" came a male voice.

"What did you think? That you could get me to trust you and then take my sister away, and hand her over to the Illyrië or something worse?"

"Wait a minute, young man!"

"You try to kill my sister and then you ask me to *wait*?" Einur shouted.

"Listen to Eldrast, Einur." It was the woman's taut voice now, and Einur hesitated. *Eldrast.* Eldrast had been his father's name, and the realisation that this man shared that name shocked him into a calmer state of mind.

"You better hurry then."

"Your sister's name was drawn the day after you were supposedly sacrificed. I'm afraid I was a little too quick in going up the tunnel to save her. The fire was barely lit; much less was the smoke thick enough to hide me. They saw me and came after us. I and my wife and Lody had to get far away from Ledmi and into as unexpected an area as we could. Who would think any refugee would make for this uninhabited desert?"

Einur didn't speak as Eldrast concluded. Instead he looked at Lody. She stared back at him, smiling.

"Is that what happened, Lody?"

She nodded.

"Are you sure?"

"The Illyrië took me away from Auntie Lyný and I was so scared, Einur! They pretended to be nice to me but I could see they were trying to hurt me. But Eldrast and Berwyn – "

Einur interrupted. "Berwyn?" He was looking at the woman now, disturbance evident in his voice.

The lantern-light glinted in Berwyn's eyes as they landed on Einur's. "That was your mother's name too, wasn't it?"

Slowly – his tongue seemed tensed up, and the words were hard to force out – he replied. "How do you know?"

"I have been around Ledmi long enough to know lots about you and many of your neighbours."

Einur continued to stare at her, and she at him. It was clear that Einur thought it more than a coincidence, but he kept still.

It was Eldrast who broke the silence. "Lody at least must sleep now. We'll have a long day of walking tomorrow and she must not slow us down."

4

THE HANDS OF THOSE YOU FEAR

They made for the Selotan Holding after that, travelling west alongside the mountains for five days and then up into and through the mountains for another two. On the eighth morning Einur awoke early and rose, rolling up the bedding he had borrowed from Eldrast. Quietly, wishing not to disturb his little sister's sleep, he crept away from the camp and up over the hump which had shaded them from the hot evening sun the night before. The hillock ended abruptly in a cliff, and Einur gazed over its edge in delight.

Far, far below him was a grey land masked

by mist. Trees rendered leafless by winter's ebbing cold stabbed up out of the layer of mist, shining dully as the sun began to dawn. On the horizon, a road struggled free from the mist, curving away out of sight. Two – no, three – wisps of smoke curled up from near the road, just before the point where Einur's eyes failed him.

For some time he watched the sun rise and the mist clear, then turned to rejoin the others. Eldrast and Berwyn had gotten up by now and were eating a simple breakfast; Lody was still sleeping deeply. Einur dropped into a crouch beside his pack and extracted one henla leaf, but as soon as Berwyn saw what he was doing she stopped him.

"Have a carrot instead, Einur. I've got a feeling you will be eating a lot of henla on this journey. No need to eat it when there's another option."

"I don't have any carrots," he said, his voice a little surly.

She laughed at him. "I'm giving you one."

"I don't need your charity," he snapped.

She wasn't laughing anymore. Now she

rolled her eyes with an irritated sigh. "Take it, Einur."

His eyes flicked up to her; her voice sounded so like his mother's had when she used to order him around. Out of a familiar instinct he reached out and plucked the carrot from her hand.

"Thanks," he muttered after a moment of silence.

She smiled before standing up and going to shake Lody awake. "It's late morning already, sweetheart," Einur could hear her murmuring to the child. "Time to get up and have breakfast. How long's it been since you've eaten a carrot?"

Einur grimaced. He wasn't yet convinced that accepting the food wasn't accepting charity. But then again it was Lody, and for Lody's sake at least he was willing to be humiliated.

A good two hours' walking, with Einur carrying Lody most of the way, brought them to the outskirts of the hamlet Einur had seen earlier. No one was about, although they could hear sounds of life within the huts. In the first hut, a child squabbled noisily with its sibling, its mother's reprimand cutting in harshly and abruptly ending the quarrel. Further down the road, someone was singing an unfamiliar ditty.

The place had a bad feel to it, Einur thought, though he kept his feeling to himself. Berwyn and Eldrast seemed unconcerned, and Lody was fully engrossed in trying to plait Einur's shoulder-length hair – it was only his arms that prevented her falling off his back considering that both her own were in use.

Lody was beginning to hum along with the unseen singer when, without warning, a figure burst out of a house to their left. It flung itself into the roadway before them and reached forward, arms stiff as an offended matron, hands hanging limply from the ends.

"Halt! Strangers from the east, halt, and give account of yourselves!"

Einur could think of nothing but trying to calm his heart, which had suffered a terrible shock at the sudden apparition. Eldrast, on the other hand, seemed not in the least ruffled, and calmly replied that they were merely passing through.

"Your names, strangers, and your business!"

"First tell us yours."

"I'm the father of this town; Father of Dale Turnsek is what my subjects call me. And now, stranger, what be your name and your lady's, and the infants'? Speak, or die!"

"Eldrast is my – " At this moment Berwyn gave her husband an urgent tap on the shoulder. "What?"

"Look behind," she hissed.

He did so, and the smallest of sighs escaped him. Far behind were ant-sized figures swarming down the side of the mountains.

"Look, father," he snapped, turning back to the old man. "Will you hide us?"

"What do I owe you that I shall put Dale Turnsek in danger?"

"Please. Just get us out of sight and tell those who come that you know nothing of my wife and the children and myself."

"I owe you nothing, youngling, and I shall not put my people in danger for the sake of unknown strangers. Go, and survive as you may on your own."

Eldrast scowled and opened his mouth to

argue further, but Berwyn placed her hand on his arm. "Eldrast, there is no time. They're getting closer."

Eldrast flashed one look behind him. "Scatter!" he growled. "Everyone go different ways, it'll make catching us harder."

Lody whimpered and clung to her brother.

"I'm not leaving Lody on her own!" Einur shouted. "She's going with me!"

"She is not," stated Eldrast tersely. "They're after you, Einur. If they get you they may leave the rest of us be, but if Lody is with you and if they capture you, she will die with you."

Slowly Einur allowed the little girl to slide down his back, she clutching at him and giving a sob as she hit the ground. He crouched in front of her.

"It's better if you go away from me for a little while, Lody, all right? I'll find you again after a time."

"Go west across the Holding, Einur. Make for the Sunset Crown – you'll see it at sunset in the western mountain range, a peak which during sunset is crowned with red. We'll all meet up at its foot. Whoever reaches the

Crown first must wait for all the rest to come."

"Look, Eldrast," began Einur, but Berwyn gave him a shove towards the south, beginning herself to run in a northward direction and Eldrast going west. Einur gave a wild glance back east; their pursuers were nearing Dale Turnsek. He began to run; south, as Berwyn's push had suggested. Lody began to follow him; he turned to her and called, "Go with Berwyn!"

Berwyn hadn't gone far, Lody could easily catch up with her...

5

SEEK KNOWLEDGE

It began to rain not ten minutes after Einur had parted from the others. Nor was it an innocent drizzle, but a hard rain that beat out a rhythm on Einur's back accompanied by the tune of thunder's discontent in the west. He merely ignored the weather, however; it was little worse than many storms he'd weathered out in the pastures. *Left foot, right foot, left foot, right.* It became almost a chanting as he plodded along. *Left foot, right foot, left foot, right.* He stopped suddenly – a light shone hesitantly through the rain. No more *left foot, right foot.* Einur began to run. He fell against the door in relief and knocked.

It opened slowly and a head peeped out. Blue eyes took in Einur from head to toe before the door opened completely.

"Come in quickly. You must be freezing."

The house was warm; a soft fire lighted the single room and gave off an amount of heat that was surprising considering the fire's size. He dropped into the closer of the two hand-carved wooden chairs which sat beside the hearth and stretched his hands as close to the flames as he dared.

The old man removed Einur's cloak from his shoulders and laid it across the table, then settled into the empty chair opposite the boy, who took time now to observe his host. He was clad in a voluminous brown robe and wore a scarf of the same colour over his head, hiding his hair. The eyes were startlingly blue and vibrant in the old face.

"I met someone not long ago with eyes just like yours," Einur found himself saying.

"Indeed?" said the man, staring at the fire.

"He told me to find the Lost – " He broke off. Why was he trusting this old fellow? There was an atmosphere of trustworthiness about him, that was why. *Makes it even worse,* he thought, *it's probably a trick.* "Never mind. It doesn't matter."

To his surprise, the old man didn't insist he finish what he'd been saying. "Where are you going, alone and in this weather?" he asked instead.

Should he say more? "I was going south," he replied vaguely.

Again no clarification was requested. "The Klendil Caves are to the south," mused the old man. "Have you ever heard that legend?"

Einur shook his head, glad to shift the conversation from himself.

"Would you like to hear it?"

"Yes, please," he muttered.

The old man pulled a blanket over his knees and began.

"Once upon a time there was a maiden of Selotan who was fair beyond words, and her hair fell flaxen to her knees. She was called Klenora, and her father's neighbour's son loved her dearly and she returned his love. But when they approached the Illyrië for leave to wed, they were refused. Yet the lovers refused to be thwarted, for they trusted not the Illyrië and believed that they were false. Thus Klenora and Mandil were wed in secret, and the Illyrië had no knowledge of their marriage. But after a time of their bliss, one jealous of Mandil's gladness betrayed their secret, and in fury the Illyrië sent the lovers to the caves of the south that they should die in sentence for their disobedience.

"And in the morning when they woke in the caverns they comforted each other, but Klenora was snatched up by a great flying creature and carried off. And Mandil pursued them, but the creature flew across a crevice. Mandil leapt blindly thinking only of his wife, but the crevice was wide and he fell into the dark with a loud cry. Thus ended Mandil, and Klenora soon after perished in the den of the beast."

Einur sat silent for a time after the tale ended. Then he asked, "Is it true?"

"Who knows?" replied the old man. "After all, neither lived to tell their tale. Yet Klenora and Mandil were real enough. Hundreds of years ago they lived in Dale Turnsek, a village some ways north of here. Perhaps you passed by it, if you are travelling south."

"I did."

"You should go back there someday, son. Their patriarch knows much lore of the Tribes."

Einur's head snapped up. "Lore of the Tribes... of the First and Second Tribes, you mean."

"Yes, he knows much of the surviving tribes; in fact, he is descended from the Chieftains of the Second Tribe. The Selotan Holding is the ancient home of the Second Tribe, you know. But he could tell much of the Third Tribe also, if you could convince him to do so."

"But the Third Tribe was lost ages ago. How does he know anything about them?"

"The lines of the Three Tribal Chieftains have the ability to see certain parts of the past, those pertaining to the other two Chieftains. Thus he knows, at least in part, where the Third Tribe went to. Their power does not allow them to see enough to do harm to each other, but the patriarch of Dale Turnsek will know whether the Lost Tribe went north, south, east, or west."

Einur's natural peasant's reserve allowed him to keep his excitement from showing elsewhere than in his eyes. "I may go back... when I've done with my business in the south."

"If you do, son, let me give you one warning. You will have to sift the truth from his embellishments – and he has no scruples concerning untruths. Be alert when you speak with him."

Einur nodded his thanks. Both sat looking into the fire for a moment, Einur's heart in turmoil within his chest. Presently the old man stood up.

"It's late. Will you be comfortable by the fire with a few blankets?"

Without waiting for an answer, he crossed to a cupboard on the other side of the room and removed a couple blankets, which he spread on the floor by the hearth.

"You don't roll in your sleep, do you?"

It took Einur a moment to realise that his host was joking. He smiled. "I'd better not."

He snuggled up in the blankets; they were warmer than his own and very soft. The fire burned low and at last the quiet flickering on his closed eyelids lulled him to sleep.

Einur thanked his host in the miserable grey morning and set off, still on his pretended route south. He waited until he was an hour's trek from the house before turning eastward. He then set his route by what was visible of the rising sun, finally wheeling to his left and hoping against hope that he'd hit Dale Turnsek again.

Gradually the weather cleared up, and by noon the sky was a rich cloudless blue. Against this colour, eventually, grey smoke rose, and Einur found that the village was now in sight. He slowed down, praying to the Great Achiel – *no, to the Master* – that the Illyrië had gone. He approached the village cautiously, sneaking around the outbuildings and huts and peeping around a corner to glare around the street before revealing himself. He now stepped lightly down the road, willing his weight not to crunch the gravel too loudly. When he came to the centre of Dale Turnsek he paused and glanced either way, thinking that one of the houses nearby must be the patriarch's. Sure enough, on the door of one directly to Einur's left was a plaque, cloud-shaped and painted garish blue. The boy walked boldly up to this hut and knocked curtly on the door.

A moment passed, and Einur was about to knock a second time when the door flew open, nearly into his face, and the grey head of the patriarch popped out – *just like the toy Father made long ago,* Einur couldn't help thinking, *the carved head that leapt out whenever Lody lifted the lid of the box.*

"What is it?" the patriarch snarled, then saw who his visitor was. His tone changed entirely. "You have returned, youngling? You have escaped your pursuers?"

"Can I come in? I'd rather not stand out here where anyone can see me. And I'd like to ask you questions about the Lost Tribe."

The patriarch stretched out a bony arm and yanked Einur through the door. "Sit, sit," he crooned. "Are you thirsty, youngling? Fresh, cold water? Ale?"

"Some water wouldn't hurt," Einur replied

as he sat down in the proffered chair.

The patriarch brought the drink in a goblet, pressing it into Einur's hands with nauseous attentiveness. He then sat across from Einur and watched the boy drink the water. As he finished, the patriarch leapt up again. "The youngling wishes to know about the Lost Tribe?"

"Yes, father, if you'd tell me."

"What do you wish to know, youngling?"

"Well, really, anything you know about them. But mostly where they are now. Do you know where they went after the Rebellion?"

The patriarch grinned, a nasty smirking grin that didn't reach his eyes. "Why do you want to know that, youngling?"

"I'm curious."

"There was a queen once with a cat that was always curious, and that same cat listened in to state secrets and ended up under the executioner's axe. That's what comes of curiosity, youngling."

Einur suppressed a laugh which almost squeezed out despite his annoyance with the old man's procrastination.

"I won't end up under the executioner's axe, father."

The patriarch eyed him. "Well if you do, don't say I didn't warn you, youngling."

"I won't, father. I promise."

"Hmph." He glared at Einur again from the corner of one eye. "Well, they went south." He smirked again. "South, through the Klendil Caves." Still another smirk. "And I can't see any more of them once they went underground."

"South?"

The patriarch's old body shot forward toward Einur and his hands grabbed the young man's shoulders. "Why?"

"Why what?"

"Why the Lost Tribe? Why not the First Tribe? Why not the Second Tribe? Did you know that I'm the rightful Chieftain of the Second Tribe, youngling?"

Einur tried to pull back – the patriarch's long nails were sending panic through the nerves of Einur's shoulders. "Wouldn't any boy be interested in a mystery like that?"

"Not so interested as to leave his home in search of answers!"

Einur gave a final wrench of his body and extricated himself from the old man's grasp. Before the patriarch could make a move Einur flung himself before the door of the hut. "Thanks for telling me what you did, but I have to go find my sister now."

The patriarch squealed and darted towards him, but the young man ducked out the door and was far down the road before the old one could do anything to stop him.

6

LET NOT YOUR HEART BE TROUBLED

*W*hy are you still going south?

Because finding the Lost Tribe is my job, not finding Berwyn and Eldrast again.

How about finding Lody?

Einur winced. That spot was sore.

"Because she won't be safe with me," he said aloud, hoping that hearing the words would convince him. "No telling what I might get into."

And I don't guess Berwyn and Eldrast will be worried or anything when you don't turn up?

"I'll go when I've searched the caves, all right!" he shouted. The words ended abruptly as they were absorbed into the open space, and Einur's ears were left with a strange feeling of sudden deafness. "They'll wait for me!"

How do you know?

"Just shut up, would you? I'm going to the caves!"

His conscience tried to speak again, but this time he forced it into silence.

Bewildered by the fact she was suddenly on her own, Lody simply ran: on and on and on. She was a hearty child who'd spent most of her life playing outdoors, and she knew she could run a long time before she had to stop and rest. Though she was only eight, she fully realised what the consequences of slowing would be – and she was terrified of the Illyrië.

She looked back once to ensure no one was in sight. All was clear; she was utterly alone in the middle of the plain. If she squinted, she could now see the shapes of the mountains in the distance, but nowhere else she looked was there anything visible but the flatness of the plain, the drying grass underfoot.

Her breath finally caught up to her and she gasped raggedly a few times, the fourth gasp turning into a great sob. She let herself fall onto the grass and wept, her tears bitter with fear and confusion and loneliness. When the sobs ended she curled into a ball and tried not to think of herself alone in the neverending expanse.

"Those were tears a child should never have had to weep," someone said, and Lody found herself gathered into motherly arms.

" *Fear not, for you shall see*
Under salt sea they be."

"What do you mean?" murmured Lody, not wanting to move from her comforting position in the woman's embrace.

The woman pulled back and set Lody before her. "I cannot tell you more clearly, sweetheart. But remember my rhyme. It will help you find your brother."

New tears sprang to Lody's eyes. "Where is Einur?"

"You'll find him in time, dear. But now you have your own journey to make, separate from his. There is much strength in you, Aloden

Landman, if you but search it out. Only once you discover your own strength can you return to your brother and stand beside him in your true place."

Lody's lower lip trembled as a new wave of confusion and desolation engulfed her small soul. The woman stood, and the little girl darted towards her. "Please..." The woman smiled at Lody, her figure wavering a little at the edges. "Don't leave me all alone!"

The wavering spread across the woman, and she faded away.

"Don't leave me alone again!"

Once more Lody sank to the ground weeping, weeping so hard she barely heard the words on the wind.

You are never alone.

Some instinct led Einur straight to a dell at the foot of one mountain. Intertwining branches of two trees formed a gateway. He was trembling as he stepped between the huge old trunks, yet he had no idea why. His quavering continued as he sidestepped blocks of carved stone that had fallen onto the sandy ground. Before him, straight ahead, was a perfectly rectangular aperture, five feet high, that looked like a portal into the void, so dark was it beyond. Fear overtook him and he looked to his left, admiring what he supposed to be representations of the lovers Mandil and Klenora, chipped into the stone walls encircling the dell.

He looked back to the doorway. It was so black within that it almost seemed to invite him to step through and let it wrap him in itself. Yet why should he feel so afraid? Surely the Master's hand would guide him through, he reasoned; but he was so unused as yet to the thought of guidance by the Master of the Harmony rather than that of the Great Achiel, that it almost seemed to him that he'd rather the Great Achiel led him through.

What could it hurt? he asked himself. Ignoring the reproach that came from deep inside him, he raised his arms to the sky as he had been taught, bowed his head, and spoke the prayer for protection which he'd been taught as a young child. This ritual completed, he stepped boldly through the doorway.

At once the darkness swirled around him and, glancing back, no light from outside showed to brighten the cave, for all he was but one step in. His legs shook, and he prayed the prayer for protection a second time.

The night grew blacker.

A third prayer he made to the Great Achiel, and the night was tangible, stretching out with dark fingers to snatch the life from Einur's soul.

"Help me!" he cried out, panicked. "Forgive me, Master. Grant me your protection, and drive out the evil spirit of Achiel."

Instantly the unnatural night fled away, and sunlight streamed through the opening and lit up the cave. Einur sighed shudderingly and dared a glance down the tunnel. The light didn't reach very far, and beyond its extent there was merely more black – not oppressive black as before, but black nonetheless. And what could he do for light? He had neither tinderbox nor torch.

Did you not say that you trust me?

Einur walked into the dark.

Somehow once he was there, it was no

longer so dark: there was a glow somewhere ahead of him which, no matter how long he travelled, remained the same distance from him. It was this glow that he followed whenever he came to a fork in the passage. Once, just to see what would happen, he did attempt going down the fork not marked by the glow; but he was not far down this new passage before a vile smell assailed him and a wisp of green mist swept around his head. A memory of the mist that'd seeped through the trapdoor behind the Temple surfaced and he panicked, groping his way back to the fork and stumbling down the right passage to escape from the mist.

He had no way of knowing how long he had been in the cave, but his stomach finally insisted it was time to stop and eat. He did so, very briefly – only a single leaf, as he couldn't tell when he might come to the end of the caves. This sparse meal completed, he scrambled up and followed the glow once again.

Abruptly he ran into something. Whatever it was, it was invisible but physical, as he discovered by patting all over it trying to find a way through. There was none, however. In despair he leaned back against the barrier, and suddenly it moved. The movement was really no more than a budge, but it was encouraging, and he tried leaning against it a second time. Again it slid a tiny bit. Einur adjusted his feet to his body's new position, and continued reclining against the hidden wall. In turn it continued moving backwards.

I guess the glow's telling me to go slow, he reasoned, enjoying the chance to rest somewhat. He let his thoughts wander to Lody. He still felt guilt at leaving her, but she'd be safer with Berwyn and Eldrast. Surely she'd caught up with them by now. She was a smart girl.

Then Einur tumbled over backward with a squawk of surprise that echoed throughout the passage.

Delicately he picked himself up and felt behind him. The barrier was gone. He edged back the way he had come, wondering if maybe the barrier had been to protect him from something. Then an instinct warned him that some danger was ahead, and he dropped to hands and knees and crawled forward, ever so slowly. And one of his hands slipped over into nothing.

Shaking, he leapt away from the drop, and made a hasty retreat in the direction of the glow. Presently he observed that its light was steadily increasing, and at last he came into an open space which was filled with light streaming from the centre of the domed roof. Straight ahead of him was a relatively narrow crevice of perhaps forty foot-lengths' width, spanned by a bridge crudely built of scraps of wood. To Einur, the construction looked shaky and very unsafe; yet, glancing around in the blessed light, there seemed no other way to cross the crack, which extended from end to end of the dome.

"Nothing else for it," he muttered, and stepped onto the bridge. It swung slightly as he cautiously shuffled across, watching intently for rotten or missing planks. Not until he'd actually set foot on solid stone again did he recognise how utterly exhausted his body was. He made for a spot at the side of the dome near the passage leading away, and arranged his blanket to create a cozy sleeping area. Curling into it, Einur fell fast asleep.

7

WHAT TOMORROW BRINGS

Einur dreamed of nigh-silent footsteps,
bewildered whispers, and long underground marches, but he was far too
tired to wake and investigate. Each time his
mind suggested he'd slept long enough, his
body protested vehemently – and it was always
his body that won the battle. It was very likely
more than a day and night before he at last
woke, to find himself no longer in his little
nook, but tucked into a bed so small that his
legs were bent up in order to fit onto it. His
knees, he discovered, were painfully cramped,
and he unfolded them to awkwardly hang off

the end of the bed. He laughed merrily at the thought of what he must look like, then realised that he had not laughed in such fashion in all his memory.

Unaccountably mirthful, he rolled out of bed, laughing again at the ridiculously undersized nightshirt he was wearing. It barely reached halfway to his knees, and whoever had put him into it had left Einur's hose on him to remedy the nightshirt's defects. He saw the rest of his clothes lying across the back of a midget-sized chair, and fought his way out of the nightshirt to dress himself properly.

At this point something scurried into the chamber and began excitedly squeaking. Einur stared at it in shock. It was perhaps – *perhaps* – a foot and a half high, but certainly no more and probably several inches shorter. The creature was jabbering away in its tiny voice and gesturing in a frenzied fashion with its hands that were smaller than a newborn infant's. It was impossible not to smile, and this Einur did. The thing paused for one moment, then resumed its lilliputian tirade.

More footsteps; a second midget pattered

into the room, saw Einur, and joined in the ranting. Finally both stopped, looked away from Einur and at each other, discussed something between themselves for a moment, then darted up to the boy and began leaping up, apparently attempting to reach his hands. He crouched down and allowed them both to catch hold of one of his small fingers, the only one they could grasp with their own hands. They began bounding towards the doorway, and Einur waddled along with them, still squatting. In this way the trio progressed down a well-lighted corridor ending in a cavern hung with myriads of lamps of various colours.

The two dwarves pulled Einur up the centre of this cavern until he stood before a kind of throne on which sat another of the creatures. This one was unbelievably tiny, even smaller than the first two. A fourth and fifth stood on either side of the throne, little battleaxes projecting a miniature defiance into the air. Einur's escorts bowed deeply from the waist, and Einur thought it best to do the same. The foot-high creature on the throne surveyed the boy for some time, then slipped off its perch and scampered up to him.

"Thou hast woken, O mine guest; and hast slept well?"

The archaic words threw Einur for a second, but he recovered and reassured the creature that he had indeed slept well.

"I am called – " it pronounced the word *called* in two syllables – "Hiveningr, King of the Naha'k, this my people. And thy name, O mine guest, is..."

"Einur," he said. "My name's Einur."

"Einooor." Hiveningr rolled the name across his tongue. "Uncouth it is, methinks, yet an honest ring it soundeth to mine ears. What is thy quest, O mine guest?"

Einur replied with a second question. "How long have your people lived around here?"

"It is seven long centuries since mine sire hath died, and seven long centuries since I myself hath ruled the Naha'k. Yet long ages before my people hath lived and died in these caves, O mine guest."

"Were they here when the Third Tribe passed through?" asked Einur eagerly.

Hiveningr observed him shrewdly. Clearly his hospitality extended only to a certain point, after which he would defend his secrets dearly. "Why dost wish to know of the Tribe that was lost? Wishest thou them harm?"

"No! No harm. I've been sent to find them."

The little king circled Einur, eyeing him in suspicion all the while. "And who hath sent thee to stir up the woe of a past age?"

How much can I tell? "One named Eigion told me what to do."

Hiveningr's eyes kindled, but his demeanour calmed. "No love for Eigion hold I or my people. Yet followeth he the Master of the Harmony, and for this I trust the one he sendeth." He scrambled back onto his throne, careless of any and all dignity. "Fifty hundreds of years since did Eriand lead the Third Tribe into our home, in the time of my father's father's father's father. And fifty hundreds of years since did mine people lead the Third Tribe to the southern side of these the Naha'k Caves, bereft of Eriand their king. This, O mine guest, is the tale I tell to thee of the Tribe that was lost."

"They left without the king? Why? He can't have died." If he *had* died...

"Nay, O mine guest, Eriand died not. The creatures of the cave air did take him."

"In other words, he died."

Mild irritation revealed itself momentarily on the king's face. "Nay, for have I not said that Eriand died not? For the safety of the king did they take him, for traitors there were within his group: those who saith they did follow Eriand, but in their hearts they were false and would betray him to his enemies. Thus the creatures did fly him to safety."

"Did he get back to the Tribe later?"

"This I know not, O mine guest."

"Do you know which way the Tribe went when they got out of your caves?"

"Westwards they went, O mine guest, towards Sarhadë."

"To the Sea..." Einur murmured, thinking of the fish carved on Eigion's staff.

"And now, O mine guest, if thou hast no more questions, a table hath been set for thou and me. Wilt thou eat, for thou hast tasted neither food nor wine for the course of a day?"

"I could eat a whole sheep," said Einur.

Einur was seated at Hiveningr's left hand, and spent most of the mealtime listening to the high-pitched nattering of the King and the wizened Naha'k at the King's other hand. The food, although exotic, was delicious, and Einur was hungrier than he'd realised. He cleared his plate in short order, then leaned back and groaned contentedly.

Hiveningr's attention turned to him at the noise. "Ah, and hast eaten well, O mine guest?"

Einur could only nod. He was so full that his stomach felt tightly stretched, and he didn't feel like speaking aloud.

"Mine adviser hath a thing that he desireth me to tell thee, as he doth not speak thy tongue."

Shoot, Einur almost replied – it was an expression Ledmians used, meaning 'go ahead'. He caught himself in time, remembering it was vulgar and Hiveningr wouldn't understand. Instead, he said, "I am listening."

"Gashagr mine adviser hath lived six

thousand years, several times the span of the lifetime of most Naha'k. He hath reminded me that when Eriand did desire to leave our realm, Gashagr did lead him from the mountains and to a region of safety."

"Where was that?"

"I know not, O mine guest."

"Can't Gashagr tell you?"

Seemingly reluctantly, Hiveningr turned to the ancient Naha'k and gabbled something. Looking back at Einur, he said, "Gashagr is willing to lead thee to this place, O mine guest, but he does warn thee that thou shalt be in danger, mayhap, if thou followest him."

"I don't care, I just want to find Eriand's descendants."

The King conveyed this to Gashagr, then told Einur, "On the morrow, O mine guest, thou shalt leave in company with Gashagr."

Einur found the sunlight surprisingly bright as he stepped out the southern entrance to the Klendil Caves, little Gashagr muttering from his place within Einur's backpack. The two couldn't converse, for the Naha'k spoke no more than a couple words of the Kelyanic tongue, and Einur nothing at all of the Naha'k. However, Gashagr was naturally talented at communicating through gestures, and his companion was quickly learning. He now slowly spun, one arm out and first finger pointing. North... west... south... east... Gashagr struck him lightly on the side of the head as he faced east.

"East it is," said Einur, and set off.

Periodically Gashagr would hit Einur in the head again to indicate a necessary change in direction, but for the most part he let the boy go straight, the now-setting sun warming their backs. As twilight fell, Gashagr pulled Einur's hair. Puzzled by the new signal, Einur stopped short and swivelled his neck round to see him. The old Naha'k put his hands together and pillowed his cheek on them. Understanding, Einur veered off his course towards an old oak standing some ways off. Here he removed his pack and lifted Gashagr out. The Naha'k stood and stretched, then curled up on the ground with his eyes closed.

Einur took his blanket out of his pack and contemplated it for some moments. There was only one, and the night was like to be cold... Gashagr was old, though. Einur sighed, went to Gashagr, and tapped him on the shoulder. One eye opened. Einur held up the blanket.

Gashagr sat and shook his head vigorously. He paused, then, pointing to himself, he shook his head again, then hugged himself and pretended to shiver. Once more he pointed to himself and shook his head.

"I get it. You don't get cold." Einur nodded, smiled, and moved a distance from the Naha'k to make his own bed.

He dreamt of being abominably cold, of shivering uncontrollably, and then of a delightful heat stealing across his body. His dreaming mind went to Efrix and the dragon's familiar warmth, and Einur snuggled closer into his blanket.

8

HE IS A KING

When Einur woke he still felt as though Efrix were next to him. He rolled over lazily, the warmth of his dreams still enveloping him, and then he nearly jumped out of his skin. Beside him lay a great dragon, slightly smaller than Efrix had been yet huge nonetheless. Einur rolled out of his blanket and stood observing the creature, wondering where in Kelyan it could've come from. Then he saw a man on the dragon's other side, still sleeping. *All right then, fellow travellers it is.*

"Hello there," he said tentatively.

The stranger snorted twice and one hand flew out in a convulsive spasm, striking the dragon. It too woke, a flame lighting up its eyes in a manner that Einur remembered well. *It was right to obey Eigion...* he mused... *but I still kind of miss Efrix.*

"Ho, friend!"

The cheery tones called Einur back and he scowled at the stranger. "Where'd you come from?"

Einur's own tone of voice, the opposite of the stranger's and packed full of suspicion, didn't dampen the other man at all. "We came upon ya last night, Gamkal an' I, pretty late. An' I thought to myself, why don't we travelers stick together, thought I? Four's better'n two in a fight, an' one o' ya not much more'n a baby from what I kin see."

"He's not a baby, he's six thousand years old," said Einur defensively. "Why do you have a dragon?"

The man gave him a puzzled look. "And why not? Hasn't everyone had dragons for mounts these last five thousand years?" He glanced at Gashagr. "'Cept maybe him, 'twouldn't surprise me, if you're not laughin' last on me 'bout him havin' six thousand years true an' for sure."

"Just 'cause everyone does it doesn't mean it's right," said Einur, surprising himself at his ready defence of Eigion's statement... *On your quest against evil, no dragon is a friend of yours.*

"Well, ain't yar a contradictin' feller, my friend. An' what's your name?"

"Tell me yours first."

"Contradictin' *an'* distrustin'! Call me Angilan, friend, an' what'll I call ya?"

"Einur."

"An' what's your little friend's name? The old feller?"

"Gashagr."

"High-fancy name for a little feller like that. What's wrong with him, friend Einur? He get squashed or somethin'?"

"You don't like his height?"

"Don't have a care for what siza boots he wears, Einur, my friend. Mere curious wonderin' is what gets to Angilan, that's what."

"Well, he's just a kind of dwarf. Don't see

how it matters more than that."

"All right, all right! I'll keep to myself if you're seein' it like that. Ya gonna wake him up or somethin'? Wouldn't mind meetin' him."

"He doesn't speak our language."

"Well now, ain't that special? All right then, like I said, I'll keep to myself. Where're you two goin'?"

"I don't know."

"An' ya actually mean that, don't ya," stated Angilan, peering into Einur's face. "I kin see it in your eyes you're not laughin' last."

"He's just leading me."

Angilan leaned around Einur and looked at Gashagr's tiny sleeping form again. He laughed. "He's leadin' ya, is he?"

"That's right." Belligerently, Einur stared straight back at Angilan.

"You two goin' east? Or don't ya know?"

"East is the way he told me yesterday."

"I'll tell ya what, my friend. I'm goin' east too. Why don't you two hitch a ride on Gamkal wi' me an' I'll put ya down wherever your friend says. You'll get somewheres some faster."

Einur considered. Could it be so wrong to

trust a dragon just this once, just to get to a possible clue a little faster? Because Angilan was right, it would be 'some faster' to fly. *Surely it must be okay*, he thought.

"Thanks. I think we will."

"Ya better wake yer little friend and have some sort o' breakfast. Gamkal's kinda restless in the mornings."

Not ten minutes later Einur was helping Gashagr into his pack. He heaved the weight onto his back and crossed to where Angilan was waiting with Gamkal. The little Naha'k immediately seemed to have a panic attack. A torrent of gibberish poured out of his mouth and he waved his short arms frantically.

"It's okay, Gashagr," said Einur, twisting around and smiling and nodding to his companion. "It's just for a ways, so we don't have to walk so far."

Gashagr continued protesting, but Einur ignored him and climbed up behind Angilan. The Naha'k's size prevented him from doing anything to stop Einur, and once they were high off the ground he gave up and fell silent. Einur rubbed his ears meditatively – the high-pitched jabbering had given him an earache, and now that he couldn't change his mind about riding the dragon he felt as though it had been a foolish idea to accept Angilan's offer.

He peered downwards, but the plains were fast disappearing and all he could see were the mountains to his left. He shrugged and turned to Gashagr, gesturing to show that when they needed to land, Gashagr should signal. The Naha'k regarded him sullenly, but Einur could tell he understood.

They followed the mountains for hours, crossing the northeast corner of Merlën Forest around noon. Now Gamkal flew across the mountains, and Einur realised how close they were to Ledmi. He frowned and looked back at Gashagr, who stared straight back at him. With a questioning glance, Einur pointed at him, then at himself, and finally at the ground. Gashagr shook his head, frowning. Einur faced ahead again, trying not to worry. Why should he anyways? They were going to pass over Ledmi and keep going east, weren't they?

He turned his mind to Lody instead, but almost immediately was disturbed by Angilan tapping on his shoulder.

"There's a village down there," he said, pointing downwards. "Ya wanna pop in and take a rest?"

Einur's hair went flying, so vehemently did he shake his head *no*.

"Why not? There ain't another one for a while."

"I just... I'd really rather not. We should keep going. I want to get to wherever Gashagr's leading me."

Angilan shrugged, then nearly shot over Gamkal's head. The dragon had plunged headfirst towards the ground.

"Stop it! Stop it!" Angilan yelled, grabbing onto his saddle just in time to keep his seat. "What're ya doin'?"

Einur looked downward and his heart nearly stopped. Directly below them was the Temple, and Gamkal was heading straight towards it. Gashagr was talking again and pointing urgently towards the village.

"Stop it!" Angilan was still yelling at the dragon, but Gamkal paid no attention at all.

"Can't you stop him?" cried Einur, terror

plain in his voice.

"Nope!"

He closed his eyes and prayed, Gashagr's little voice still piercing his skull.

Then he was tumbling head-over-heels, the wind screaming in his ears. He flailed, illogically attempting to grab onto something that would break his fall. But it was useless. He struck the ground with a thud and lay curled in a ball, moaning.

A foot hit the grass beside his ear and his eyes flew open as he rolled instinctively away. "Keep back!" he gasped.

"You all right, Einur?"

"*Gernhr?*"

"Why're you right here by the Temple? Are you crazy?"

"Idiot dragon shook me off," Einur said tersely. He slipped off his pack to check on Gashagr, but he'd disappeared. "Gashagr?"

The Naha'k's head popped up. He'd hidden in the softness of Einur's blanket. The young man sighed in relief. "You okay?"

Gashagr merely grimaced at him.

Gernhr was staring. "What on this good

earth is that?"

"This is Gashagr." Einur looked at Gashagr and pointed to Gernhr. "Gernhr," he said, and Gashagr nodded. "He's a Naha'k."

"A what?"

"They live in the caves. The Klendil Caves. He was gonna show me..." He stopped, thinking it was probably best not to speak of his task in the open, especially so near the Temple.

"Show you what?"

"Tell you later. When we're alone."

Gernhr raised his eyebrows. "What've you been up to? Have you really been all the way to the Selotan Holding? In the Klendil Caves?"

"Yes. Can you sneak me into your longhouse or something? Or maybe not. We can go up to the Landman pastures."

"No, that's not safe. The Illyrië confiscated all your land and belongings. They say it'll partly make up for the loss of you and Lody both." He flushed. "You probably didn't know about Lody getting picked."

"Actually, I did – she caught up to me a few days ago."

"Then where is she now?"

It was Einur's turn to redden. "We had to separate up by Dale Turnsek... that's a village in the Selotan Holding. But it's a long story, and we shouldn't be standing out here by the Temple. Where's a safe place we could talk?"

"Not many places. The Illyrië actually set up a sentinel at each of the entrances to Ledmi after you two disappeared. They seem really worried about something. But if we keep heading out of town, we can sit out in the meadows past the Temple."

The boys continued talking as they cautiously crossed the fields east of Ledmi. Einur gave his friend some of the more general details of what he'd been doing, even unbending as far as to tell Gernhr what he was supposed to be looking for. When he heard his friend was looking for the King of the Lost Tribe, Gernhr half laughed, then frowned.

"What's the matter?"

"Well, I was gonna laugh at how silly it sounded, but then I couldn't. Something seems right about you looking for them." Gernhr stopped speaking and frowned again. He was silent for several minutes. Then he asked, "Can we run?"

"What for?"

"I want to tell you something badly... but I can't do it till we're absolutely alone."

"You still okay back there, Gashagr?" asked Einur. He turned to the Naha'k, who grinned. "I'm gonna run for a bit."

"Why do you keep talking to him? He can't understand you or anything."

"It just feels wrong to never actually *talk* to someone." He looked at Gashagr again.

"Eriand."

The name was strongly accented when Gashagr pronounced it, but easily understandable.

Einur's heart skipped a beat. "Did you leave him around here?" Gashagr seemed confused, so Einur used actions. "Eriand?" he inquired, sweeping his arm around.

Gashagr nodded.

Einur glanced at Gernhr, who appeared to be far away in thought. "Gernhr?"

"Einur, I really need to talk to you."

He squashed his longing to find out more

about Eriand and the odd coincidence of his having come to Ledmi. For now, Gernhr came first. "Race you to that copse of trees?"

Gernhr followed Einur's pointing finger. "I can always beat you."

They took off at the same moment, but Gernhr beat Einur by about a foot. Einur dropped onto the grass laughing hysterically. "I'll beat you someday, I promise!"

Gernhr stuck out his tongue. "We'll see!"

Einur stuck out his own tongue in return. "Now tell me. What's so urgent?"

"Well... I had the strangest dream the other night. There was this one young fellow with a crown on his head – " Abruptly he broke off and threw a look behind him. "What're you doing sneaking up on us?" he cried.

"Nothin', son!" Angilan wore a hurt expression. "Merely tryin' to see if my friend Einur's all right. That were a nasty fall ya took," he said to Einur.

"I'm fine."

"Ya sound mad."

"I'm not mad."

"Yar annoyed then."

"Yes."

"Is it somethin' I said?"

"No... Gernhr was telling me something private and I kinda wanted to hear it." Angilan had been kind, though. "But it can wait if you've got time to stay around for a bit."

"Nah, I won't keep ya from your talk, friend. Gamkal an' I hafta take off anyway, we're goin' down to Mourvh."

"I'm sorry we took you so off your course."

"It's nothin'. I'd'a probably stopped in Ledmi anyway even if ya weren't with me. I usually do when I come this way. I've got a friend here. Well, I'd better be goin'. Gamkal gets restless when I'm away too long."

"Thank you for giving us a ride," said Einur sincerely. "I really appreciated it."

"No problem. Good luck, Einur."

"Thanks. Same to you."

Angilan pushed back through the brush, and the boys watched him until he was out of sight.

"Now... you were talking about a young fellow wearing a crown."

Gernhr nodded. "The funny thing was he

reminded me of you. It definitely wasn't you, though. He didn't look much like you, though he had blond hair like yours, and maybe his nose was the same." He paused and studied Einur's nose for a while. This struck Einur as comical, and he laughed.

"You looked at his nose close enough to see that it was like mine?"

Gernhr chuckled too. "It is kinda funny, isn't it? But I couldn't help looking carefully at him. Something made me. So as I was saying, he reminded me of you even though he didn't look much like you. His clothes were real old-fashioned, and he was herding sheep."

"He was wearing a crown and herding sheep?" Einur was incredulous.

"Yup. That was another part of it that was so odd. And maybe it's part of the reason he made me think of you, him being with the sheep."

"Was that all?"

"Almost. Right about the end of the dream there was a woman who came running up to him, calling his name. Can't remember what his name was... it might've started with an 'a'."

"Could it've been Eriand?"

"That was it!" exclaimed Gernhr. "Eriand."

"And was he somewhere you recognised?" Einur asked, carefully regulating his excitement.

"Right up in your pastures. That's what it looked like."

"Oh my," breathed Einur.

"What?"

A realisation struck Einur full in the forehead.

"Oh."

"Einur, are you okay? You're white as a scared sheep!"

"It's not true!" Einur cried out, leaping up wildly. "It's not true!"

Gernhr grabbed his arms. "Calm down, Einur! Are you okay? What's not true? Einur, what's the matter?"

Einur stared at his friend with huge eyes. "Don't you realise, Gernhr?"

"Realise what? You're not making any sense!"

"Gernhr... I *am* the lost King."

9

WANDER ALONE

He made Gernhr stay in Ledmi.

It was too dangerous to leave, he said; the Illyrië were evidently still after him, if Dale Turnsek had been any proof. And Gernhr's parents needed him. Gernhr let himself be convinced. He'd never been much a one for pulling risky stunts; he liked to stay around home. Einur knew – he was like that himself. He'd never have accepted this mission if it hadn't been for Lody.

He lurked around the little copse all the afternoon till after dark, when Gernhr snuck back to him with food and a second blanket.

Then he left, skirting the village and going westwards again. *Towards Sarhadë*, he thought, remembering the information King Hiveningr had given him.

King Hiveningr... the thought reminded him of Gashagr, who was sleeping soundly on Einur's back. *I'll put the old Naha'k down by the entrance to the Caves*, he told himself. *No way I'm taking him all the way with me. Even if he wanted to. Which he doesn't.*

Eventually he had to stop to sleep. Under the watch of the mountains he slept deeply until the brightness of the rising sun woke him. Gashagr was making a breakfast of one of Gernhr's loaves of bread, and Einur wearily joined him.

"We don't have to go up into the mountains," he said as he ate, more for the sake of hearing a human voice than for Gashagr's benefit, "'cause right about here there's a valley kind of thing that goes between two of 'em. It'll make it a lot quicker getting you home. The valley will pretty much lead right into the forest, I guess. The Merlën Forest, I mean. We'll go through the northeast corner of it, the part we crossed when we were with Angilan.

Then along the mountains again till I get you back to the Caves. After that I guess I'll keep going towards the Sea."

Gashagr was eating greedily and didn't acknowledge Einur in any way. The young man gazed off in Ledmi's direction. "I kind of miss being at home. Actually, I really miss it. Even if there was always danger of me getting drawn for the sacrifice. I hate being on the run all the time. I'd far rather be up in the pasture with my sheep, or running races with Gernhr. I *am* going to beat him in a race someday, you know..." His voice faded away as he realised he might never have the chance.

He took a breath. "You done?"

Gashagr was.

"Let's be on our way."

As Einur had calculated, the valley ended at the very edge of the forest. The place was otherworldly – the ground was a mat of soft dried pine needles, and trees pierced this mat at intervals: tall, thin, twisted trees, some leaning at fantastic angles to the ground. Einur navigated the labyrinth in awe. He'd never seen anything like the early morning mist filtering through the branches high above his head.

"It's like fairies could live here," he observed to Gashagr. "And it's almost too quiet. Almost frightening, if you know what I mean. You're probably wondering why I keep talking to you when you can't understand me or anything. I guess I'm crazy. But like I said, it's too quiet in this forest. It's better if I talk."

Despite what he said, he fell silent. Talking didn't really help all that much. It was the only sound he could hear, and it made the background hush feel louder.

Three hours after coming to the end of the forest, Einur began to recognise where they were, and they soon passed the spot where they had spent the night before meeting Angilan. Finally they came to the gates of the Caves.

"You good from here?" he asked Gashagr.

The Naha'k smiled hugely and bowed several times. Awkwardly, Einur bowed in return. With a wave of his hand, Gashagr scampered through the entrance and disappeared in the dark. Einur sighed. *Alone again.* He turned his face westward and trudged on.

Wait. He stopped. *What about Lody? The Sunset Crown?* A bolt of guilt shot through him and he had to squelch it. *Too late now. Trust to the Great Ach – to the Master.*

At first he fully intended to continue the way he was going, but now he felt an unaccountable urge to turn south. He had a long argument with himself over whether or not he should follow the instinct, but finally decided it was probably best to obey it. He turned to his left and went on with the sun at his right hand.

The Merlën Forest stretched far to the west from where Einur and Gashagr had crossed a part of it, and as the sky grew dark Einur came upon the very end of the forest. The thought of spending the night on its edge disturbed him somewhat, but he was tired; he'd gotten up early and barely rested all day. He found some fallen branches and stuck them into the ground, creating a sort of hut, which gave him a feeling of greater security. Crawling into it, he snuggled into his blankets – the air was becoming chilly. But he found it impossible to rest. Yesterday's realisation was nibbling persistently at his mind.

I'm a king, he thought. *Or at least a king's descendant. Maybe not his heir. I pray not his heir. Maybe it's my mother who was descended from Eriand, so that being of a female line rules me out. I don't want to be a stupid king and live in a stupid castle! I want to go back to Lody and my sheep. I think I am the king though. I guess a person can sense that sort of thing...*

At this point he fell asleep and didn't wake until a fat raindrop landed directly on his left eyelid.

"Ow!" he yelped, and sat up hastily, only to hit his head on the top of his little hut, knocking it to pieces.

Without the hut he was entirely unprotected from the heavy rain, and he grabbed his pack and blankets and ran for the shelter of the trees. *Good thing I stayed near the forest after all,* he thought ruefully, examining his soaked luggage. *What a mess already.*

The tree branches were knit tightly together high above him, keeping the rain out, and he thankfully spread his things out on the ground. There was plenty of time for them to dry, for the rain kept up for several hours. At last it dwindled to a mere drizzle, and Einur packed up and decided to ignore what was left of the storm.

He ignored what was in front of him and instead watched the grey clouds scudding across the sky. When he was little, his father and he would sit outside the longhouse and pick out shapes in the clouds. These rain-clouds, however, had no recognisable forms. They were shapeless masses of dull wet. But Einur found he liked them. He loved dreary days; they had more personality, he thought. *If there were a strong wind, it'd be a perfect day.*

Just as he concluded this thought he tripped.

He glanced at the ground and found what had tripped him: an ancient metal ring sticking out of the ground. He bent and gave it a bit of a pull. Finding it didn't move, he used both hands and yanked. The ground gave way a little and, encouraged, he jerked at it a second time. He flew over backwards. *Twice in five minutes?*

Einur picked himself up once more, not bothering to dust off the dirt which had shot through the air and landed mostly on him, and took a look at what he'd uncovered – a chest about the same age as the ring, one foot long and half as deep. He gave its lid a tentative pluck, then one more confident, and to his surprise it opened quite easily. Within were a number of stone tablets covered in small runes. Einur spent a moment doing nothing more than gazing at them, excited beyond excitement. Whether or not this was a clue to the Lost Tribe, it would be fascinating to read so old an account. *That is, if the runes aren't too old-fashioned to make out.*

He leaned into the hole and pulled out the chest, removed the tablets. The runes were a little different from those he'd learned, but they were similar enough that he could make out what had been written.

A remnant of our Tribe, being the Third of Lo'Rien, survives. The First and Second did rebel against the Master of the Harmony and have set up a god of their own whom they worship with evil rites of child sacrifice. Our King Eriand could do no less than challenge this evil, but we have failed to prevent its spread, and our king is now gone, disappeared in the Caves of the North. We therefore flee in search of a refuge which

Here the tablet came to an end, and Einur set it aside in favour of the next one.

will hide us. The fairies of the sea have told us of a safe refuge which they will grant to us for as many years as there shall be until the Master of the Harmony sees fit to throw down the evil of the First and Second Tribes. But at this time we go south, for we have heard that there are caverns near to the Emli River which may hide us, and we wish to be unbeholden to all if we may. We bury these tablets in the hopes that someday

This tablet too ended, and Einur took up the last.

one who seeks us may find them. Perhaps the one who finds them may be our king, or his heir. Whomever you may be, I call down the highest blessings of our Master upon you. May you walk always in his light and follow his ways, rejecting the darkness of all false gods. To you and yours be all joy and peace. These runes written by the hand of Alaril, sister-son to Eriand our King.

All Einur could think as he finished was, *What if I'd ignored that feeling and kept going west?*

There was nothing he could do with the chest save rebury it, so he did this and slipped the tablets into his pack. Caverns near the Emli River? He knew of the Sacred Mines, but had never heard of anything else – though that was scarcely surprising considering he'd spent his entire life cooped up in Ledmi. The Sacred Mines, then, were the best place to begin. Surely you couldn't call that running straight into the arms of the Illyrië and their hirelings – it was so far from Ledmi, and news couldn't spread like that. One escaped sacrifice... well, two... couldn't be that important.

He didn't rest until he reached Iloaar, a town around twice Ledmi's size which sat on the bend of the river. Following the same logic as he'd used to justify the idea of approaching the Mines, he strode down the main street in full view, glorying in the feeling that he didn't have to hide himself anymore. Here and there a man nodded to him or a pretty girl gave him a bold smile. He returned the greetings exulting inwardly. Enjoying the familiar smell of the town's dragon stables, he stopped at the inn just beyond and read the sign: the Greedy Hen. *Someone evidently has a sense of humour*, he thought as he chuckled. He pulled open the heavy door and went in.

A meaty smell that was pure delight wisped into his nose and he inhaled. Now that was far better still than the reek of dragon and burning wood that had filled the street.

"What's to be tonight, young sir?"

Einur turned to his left and greeted the short woman who peered over the counter. "I'm in a bit of a bad situation here, ma'am. Can I exchange work for supper and a room for the night?"

"Now then," she said reflectively. "A room's ten coppers, and my cheapest meal's three. If you spend the rest of the evening servin' for me and then clean up after, I could see my way to lettin' you have them. You have an honest face, which isn't somethin' I see too often. Look around whilst you're workin'. You'll see. But anyways, my name's Bell. And yours?"

"Einur – my name is Einur."

Bell brightened. "If you'd come last night I could've told you that was a name I'd never heard. I feel like I heard someone sayin' your name just this mornin'. Though I can't remember what it was all about. I 'ear more talk than I care for, runnin' the Greedy Hen. Are you 'ungry?"

"'Yes' would be the truest thing I ever said."

"Well, I know no one ever worked good on an empty stomach, so I'll give you supper now if you swear you'll eat quickly."

Einur had never actually drooled over the smell of food, but he came near to it as Bell dished up a generous bowl of beef stew. He downed it within minutes; then, following Bell's orders, ran a number of meals out to patrons. The roast duck seemed a popular order tonight, and evidently a couple of the men had had too many tankards of the cider which came with it.

He plunked a plate of duck down before a copper-haired fellow in fancy clothing and began to leave when something jumped onto his shoulder and began to nibble at his hair. Einur squawked and shook the thing off. The man behind him was laughing, and Einur turned to see him fondling a thin creature with a tube-like body. Its head was incongruously small at the end of its elongated neck, and its eyes were curiously observing the young man.

"What is it?" he asked.

"It's a ferret," replied the man. "Name's Coenburg."

"It's cute," said Einur, petting Coenburg's head with one finger.

"Do you want him? He ruined my parchment the other day, so I guess I'm better off without him."

"Are you a scholar?"

The man bowed. "Scholar Elres at your service."

Einur managed an awkward bow in return. "I'm Einur."

"I'm serious, Einur, you can have him if you want him."

Einur reached out and the ferret slipped out of Elres' grasp and into Einur's hands. "I think he likes me!" exclaimed Einur, stroking the creature's fur.

"Done?"

"Done! Thank you!"

"Ei*nuuuuuur*!" shrieked Bell just then, and Einur hastily shook Elres' hand with another thanks before running back to the kitchen.

"Where can I put Coenburg?" he asked Bell, exhibiting his pet.

"Don't tell me Elres got you to take 'im," she groaned, rolling her eyes. "That ferret is nothin' but trouble, day's start to day's end. But put 'im in that cupboard there."

Einur was spent by the time the common room cleared out, long after dark. Bell lit a candle and led him to a room at the end of a passage.

"Small but comfortable," she said. "Sleep well. If'n you wake early I'll give you somethin' to eat afore you 'ave to go."

10

THEY ARE TOO STRONG

She'd never been on her own in the dark, and she cowered in as small a ball as she could make. Arms wrapped tightly round her legs and head burrowed between her knees, she tried to block the noises that crept into her unwilling ears. Morning came slowly, and when it did it discovered a tiny girl curled in the grass, sleeping exhaustedly, tear trails leading down to her chin.

Lody didn't wake till late in the morning, and even then she didn't move. It was a long time before hunger made her stand miserably up and go in search of something to eat. She'd only shared Einur's food; it was all in his own pack, and she had nothing but the gown that clung damply to her skin. Dew was only beautiful on plants.

Her first and only instinct was to head for home. Never had she seen a map, but she remembered walking toward the sunset when she was with Einur and Berwyn and Eldrast, so now she should walk the other way. But where had the sun risen? It certainly wasn't noon, if she looked at the sun, but it could be morning or afternoon. *How long did I sleep?*

She would have stayed where she was if it hadn't been for her griping stomach. She took a random direction and went in search of henla. Surely it grew here too. And it did – she found a patch not far away. She ripped up a handful of leaves and ate them all within minutes. She tore a wide strip from the bottom of her dress, then pulled up the entire patch and tied the leaves into the material. *There. That's plenty for a while.* She glanced up at the sun. It had moved higher – so yes, it was still morning. And home was that way.

Lody took a step towards the sun before

something catapulted itself into her mind.

"*Fear not, for you shall see*

Under salt sea they be."

The rhyme! And the woman had said it would help her find Einur. But where was the Sea? Should she turn around and merely trust to the Great Achiel to lead her steps? That sounded about right; it was her best plan at any rate, and she followed it.

But how in Kelyan can I cross the mountains by myself? she found herself wondering a couple hours later as she munched henla, gazing up at the peak above her. She hung her head, and it was then that she noticed the grass was trampled down as though a person had walked there. Following a trail made in this manner, she discovered it led upwards. *May as well follow it.*

When the sun sank she was near to the top of the mountain. *If only I had a blanket*, she cried softly as she huddled in the chilled air. Yet despite the cold she soon fell asleep.

"What do we do with her?"

The figure above Lody faced the other, his bright eyes questioning in the dark.

"We'd better take her."

"She better not wake up – where's that potion?"

The second figure passed a bottle to the speaker, who uncorked it and poured three drops between Lody's parted, chapped lips. The little girl gave a brief sigh and rolled over, falling into a deeper slumber. One of them picked her up, holding her like a newborn infant, and both made off towards the summit.

Light came pink in the east and Lody still slept in the arms of the figure, whose features became clear as the light grew. He sported dark hair with tints of blue, hanging half a dozen inches or so below his shoulders. His eyes were slightly odd, one shifting all over the place while the other was stationary. In contrast, his companion's appearance was handsome and open: dark blond hair which just brushed the shoulder seams of his tunic; and bright friendly blue eyes.

The trio was far past the mountain's summit by now and well on their way down the other side. In the cloudless morning, the entire Minvëloh Holding was laid out below them.

Farmland comprised much of this Holding, but directly below where the three now stood was a goodly-sized village.

"We'll be in Dale Alnwick by the time the sun's well up," stated the blond man, and the other nodded.

"Malia will take fine care of the child while we search for her brother."

They came down into the village and knocked on the first door. It was several minutes before a sleepy, cross woman opened it.

"What?"

"Haledon and I've brought the little girl."

"Well, dump her here and go away. You could've waited till later in the day, Vaal. You know I sleep late."

"That's why I brought her now. 'Tis good for you to be rousted out of bed early once in a while, Malia."

Malia's sulk grew nastier. "If you weren't my brother I'd horsewhip you good."

"Give her here, Vaal," snapped the other young man, "before you two start fighting and drop her."

Vaal slipped the girl into his companion's arms and resumed his bickering with the woman. Haledon shoved past them both into the house, located a cot, and gently laid Lody on it. She was finally showing signs of waking; he left her side and poked around in a number of cupboards before coming up with a bottle. Three drops of this one he forced into her mouth to counteract the three drops of poison, and her eyes opened.

The first thing she saw was an unfamiliar face hanging over her, and she flinched back from it.

"It's okay," he said, and she regarded him suspiciously. "I wouldn't harm a child for the rule of the world."

A small smile sneaked onto her lips. "Is Einur here?"

"That's your brother, right?"

"Yes, sir."

"He's not here now, but my friend's hoping he can join you soon."

"Are you gonna find him and tell him where I am?"

"That's what Vaal intends."

"Is that Vaal out there?" Lody pointed.

Haledon followed the line of her index finger to where Vaal and Malia were still quarrelling.

"That's right."

"Then I hope you find him, 'cause you're a lot nicer. Is she gonna take care of me?" This time she indicated Malia.

"Again, that's right."

"Can I have something to eat?"

In reply Haledon got up and fetched a loaf of bread he'd found whilst rummaging for the potion. He broke off a generous hunk and offered it to her.

She managed a shy grin. "Thanks."

He watched the little girl tear into it as though she hadn't eaten for ages. "What's your name?"

"Lody," she said with her mouth full.

"And how old are you?"

"Eight." She chewed up and swallowed a large bite. "What's *your* name?"

"Haledon." She opened her mouth once more and he anticipated her next question. "And I'm eighteen."

Lody set her bread down and counted on her fingers. "That's ten. Ten more than me."

"Good counting," he told her. "Now eat up quickly and I'll introduce you to Malia."

Without a doubt she had no refined manners, the way she gulped down the rest of her breakfast. She swung her legs off the bed and scampered ahead of Haledon to the others.

She gave Malia a disarming smile. "I'm Lody and I'm eight," she confided.

Malia glowered down at her. "Very nice," she replied, her face belying the words. "You're a morning person now, ain't you."

"I like to be up!" exclaimed Lody. "I like to say good morning to the sheep."

"Well, get inside. You'll be spending a lot of time indoors the next few days."

"Just till your brother comes," said Vaal in a syrupy tone, and Haledon flashed him an angry look. "What?"

"There's no need to go that far," muttered Haledon.

"Got a conscience of a sudden?"

Haledon turned away.

"We've got to go. You get the girl now,

Malia. Come on, Haledon."

Vaal set off, but Haledon grabbed Malia by the arms.

"You take good care of Lody, or I'll have something to say to you when I get back."

"What makes you think I wouldn't be nice to a sweet little girl like that?" she answered, her eyes not meeting his.

"How about everything?"

"That good-for-nothing stole something of mine for you to eat, right?" Lody peeked up at Malia from her seat on the bed. "Thought so. Since you're full of my fare, you can take this broom and sweep out the house. And mind you do it good, or I'll beat you."

Lody's confused expression broke down into one of hurt, but she took the broom from Malia and meekly did as told.

All day long it was the same treatment that Lody received. Twice Malia slapped her for making a small mistake, and when night came and she was finally allowed to rest, she was ordered to sleep in the backyard.

"Can't I please have a blanket?" she begged.

"You eat my food and then think you can have a blanket? What'll you ask for next, a kingdom?"

Lody crept out the back door.

She woke with a raging throat and hot forehead, yet Malia drove her harder than the day before. Lody was nigh on fire the entire day – flames tearing down her throat each time she tried to swallow, her head hot and throbbing, and tears burning the backs of her eyes, fighting to escape. For nothing more than a little relief, she let the tears go around noon when Malia refused her food, not that her throat could've borne to eat anything in the first place.

Again the night was old when she finally dropped to the mud in the yard, too spent to think of the cold. Again she was sick when she awoke, and again she was pushed past all possible limits of her strength. The tears could not be repressed, and Malia beat her for wetting the dirt floor.

The sores on her back would not allow her to lie down to rest when Malia let her go, and she stood swaying in the moonless night, weeping. Yet between sobs she thought she could hear a voice in her head, and after a while she quieted enough that she could hear it.

There is much strength in you, Alo– A hiccuping sob interrupted. *Aloden Landman, if you but search it out. Only once you discover your own strength can you return to your brother and—* The rest was lost in a fresh wave of crying at the thought of Einur.

Her mind connected these words with others, however, and she found herself singing.

" *Fear not, for you shall see*

Under salt sea they be."

"Shut up!" yelled Malia from a window above. "Can't a decent person get some sleep?"

"No," whispered Lody. "No, you can, but a decent person can't." *There is much strength in you, Aloden Landman...*

She ran into the dark.

11
WALK IN WISDOM

E inur took leave of Bell just after dawn with Coenburg enthroned on his shoulder. He'd attempted to put the ferret into his pack where he couldn't get away, but Coenburg had made such a fuss he finally gave up and trusted to the ferret's quick affection for him. He spent most of his time preening or nibbling on Einur's ear, but when Einur took a break at midday he was off before Einur could stop him, towards the river to investigate. He dabbed his paw in the water, glanced back at Einur, and then slid in. Einur watched him swim – he brought up his front paws to his chin, his nose just peeping out of the water. He didn't spend long swimming, and soon came back to beg for his own share of luncheon.

The day was so clear that Einur could see across the river and far across the River Plains, enclosed by the Emli and Storm Rivers. They were vibrantly green and lush; Einur could practically feel the grass's softness on his weary feet. Presently, however, the Plains were obscured by the thick steam that rose from the river here. *Must be nearing the Mines*, he thought, *for the water to be that hot.* He elected to turn aside and head away from the river. As he did so, Coenburg flew off his shoulder, scuttled back to the water, and curiously batted at the steam. He stuck his paw in but drew it out at once as though burned, and ran back to Einur, who picked him up and carried him in his arms.

Before long Einur came in sight of a group of little cottages. Outside one sat an old man chipping away at a block of wood. Einur approached him and bowed.

"Good afternoon, father. How goes it?"

The old man raised his eyes to Einur's. "Fair

enough, my thanks to you, son."

"May I ask how far to the Sacred Mines?"

An arm swept out, pointing. "Five minutes' walk that way, and haven't I myself walked that path times aplenty?"

"You were a miner?"

"That I was, curse the day I came."

"Then do you know how long the caves have been there?"

"If you believe the Illyrië, they were carved out over a thousand years by my like. Sometimes I have my doubts about that."

"Why's that, father?"

"Caves look far and away too old for a thousand years. If you want my thought, I'd say they go back five times that."

"That old?"

"Indeed." He made his body stand. "Now if you'll forgive me, son, I've a need to go." A second's silence, then a reluctant addition. "May the Great Achiel keep you."

Einur inclined his head. "And the Master keep you," he murmured.

The old man gave him a furtive glance. After a screaming pause, he opened his mouth.

"What?"

"Nothing," replied Einur, turning away.

The other tripped towards him and clutched his arm.

"Who are you?"

He wanted to ask, *Does it matter?* and walk on, but respect for the man's age prevented him. "Einur's my name. But I will leave you to your business, father."

"No! Don't go."

Einur looked at him. The old man's eyes fastened on his face. "Where are you from?"

"North."

He went down on one knee. "The Master bless you, my King!"

Einur shook his head in disbelief. "Why do you call me that?"

"Do you not know?"

Again Einur began to shake his head, but it turned into a nod of assent. "I do know."

"Don't go to the Mines, lord – they're watching for you."

"Why in Kelyan should they *watch* for me?"

"The story's spread across the land, to hear tell. Did you not know that the Illyrië figured out who you were and purposely drew your name because of it? The messenger from your home told the tale that you were a lunatic who believed you were the lost King and had managed to slither out of their hands when they detained you; but my friends and I worked out a more likely tale. Now fly, lord!"

"All blessings upon your head, father. But I must find the Lost Tribe, and if there is a chance of their having come to the Mines I must act on it."

"My lord, the Mines have never been inhabited. You will find nothing."

"What then of the tablets I found stating that they were searching out caverns near to the Emli?"

"You found tablets?" Excitement flashed like lightning from the old man's eyes.

In answer Einur shrugged off his pack and, finding the tablets, held them out. The old man snatched them and scanned them carefully. Then he shook his head.

"My lord, this seems a true account, but whether it is or is not, you will find nothing in the Mines but capture by your enemies. This you cannot risk. Our tribe needs the return of their king, and you have no heir. Go and ask counsel of the sea fairies that are mentioned by Alaril. If then you find the Tribe never came to Sarhadë, come back to the Mines – but first try the sea."

"I'll do as you say, father. Will you come with me?"

The old man hung his head. "Alas, lord, I can no longer make a journey of such length. The Mines have wearied my body too far."

"Then once again, the Master bless you. Farewell."

Taking Einur's hand, the old man kissed it. "I feel young since I have seen you, lord. The Master keep you."

Reluctantly Einur turned aside for the last time, waving his hand to the other. He set a straight course west, instead of south to the Mines, with the sun burning on his face.

Newly-found determination pushed Lody on in an unbroken trek of four hours before her body insisted on rest. Even then she sat only half an hour, watching the sun rise. As the soft caressing warmth breasted the mountains behind her she got to her feet and went on.

Morning was not yet gone when Sarhadë came in sight. Up to the far horizon the Sea was a deep teal colour, where it became dark blue. The sky was pinkish against the water; higher it held a slight yellow tinge which gradually blended into a pale blue. Bordering a sandy beach running down to the water's edge stood a guard of trees, delightfully green next the sky. Just a few wispy clouds marred the perfection of the blue.

Lody caught her breath and stared before she began to run. Her bare feet kicked up sand as she flew across the beach, arms outstretched in exultation. At last she dropped to her knees in the shallow water.

"It's so beautiful!" she laughed, all pains wholly forgotten.

And forgotten her troubles remained while she bathed and splashed around – the welts from Malia's beatings had scabbed over, preventing the salt from stinging. She dried herself by running once more across the sand,

and then lay down in the grass to nap, utterly fatigued by her sleepless night and long exercise.

Yet even now she wasn't allowed to sleep. Voices appeared out of nowhere and Lody's heart went wild. She dashed for the cover of a sparse bush and peeped out as the voices came nearer.

"The Most Illustrious expects him to be up to either Putae or Anglesea within the next couple of days. He's got watches on the gates of both cities but as we've seen, the boy's as good as all peasants at sneaking around."

Lody shivered as Vaal's familiar blue-black hair and uncouth scent swished past her. She turned her head ever so slightly to look up – and her eyes stared straight into Haledon's. His widened. Unwittingly her expression implored him to keep still.

Haledon moved inconspicuously to a position between Vaal and Lody's bush.

"Sestimon – "

"How dare you call the Most Illustrious by his name?"

"The Most Illustrious then, what should I

care?"

"You should care if you *don't* care to be his next sacrifice to the Great Achiel."

"Someone reported the boy was heading for Iloaar the other day."

"Did he get there?"

"No. Not yet."

"Did the Most Illustrious send someone to pick him up if he gets there?"

"He did say there was some scholar fellow who would set a trap."

Are they talking about Einur? Lody thought all of a sudden, and couldn't repress a sharp fidget. Vaal's eyes darted towards the bush.

"Something in there, Haledon?"

Haledon turned around and pretended to check between the leaves. His eyes met Lody's and he frowned, mutely forming a 'Sh' with his lips. She gave a little nod.

"Nothing. Must've been a squirrel or some such."

"Well, I'm turning off; gonna stick around in Anglesea. If the kid's smart he'll head for Anglesea as it's closer to Iloaar than Putae. You're gonna pick up the little girl, I suppose?"

"That was my plan."

"I'll meet you in Anglesea in a week if nothing else comes up."

"See you then."

Vaal strode away. The moment he was out of sight Haledon bent down, taking Lody's hand and pulling her out of the bush.

"How in Kelyan did you get all the way down here?"

"Malia beat me and I ran away."

Haledon swore. Lody gasped. He looked remorseful. "I'm sorry. I was angry."

"They kill people when they use the Great Achiel's name lightly," whispered Lody.

He reached out and tugged her hair. "Hey, no one but you heard me. And I..." He stopped and she flashed a sweetly inquisitive look in his face.

"You what?"

"Never mind, it's not something I should say aloud."

"You already used the Great Achiel's name wrong," she pointed out.

He grinned. "I'll tell you some other time, Mistress Curious. Did no one ever tell you curiosity killed the cat?"

"My ma used to say that sometimes."

"There you go."

She changed the subject with the ease of a child. "Is Vaal looking for Einur?"

Haledon's lips tightened. "That's right."

"I hope he finds him soon, even though I wanted you to find him, not Vaal. But I miss him so it doesn't really matter."

"Well, I hope we'll be able to join him soon, but right now we're going to take a ship across the Sea."

She leapt up with a squeal of delight. "*Really?*"

He laughed. "Yes, really! I'm not teasing!"

Lody clapped her hands. "When?"

"It's just a little walk along the beach. We can get there before the sun goes down, and I'll introduce you to my friend and his sister."

"Are they nice?"

"Much nicer than Vaal." Haledon smiled at Lody and she smiled back.

Slipping her hand into his, she pranced off at his side.

12

FROM THEIR RAVAGES

The first thing Einur saw when he neared Putae late in the afternoon two days later was Eldrast's familiar tall figure. *Lody!* his mind shouted, and he streaked towards the man and his wife.

His heart slowed when he found them alone. "Where's Lody?"

"What do you mean, where's Lody?" Eldrast was clearly baffled.

"You had her! She's okay, isn't she?"

"We never – " Eldrast began, but Berwyn interrupted him. She darted at Einur, caught him by the shoulders, and shook him.

"What have you done with her?" The look in the woman's eyes was terrible. "What have you done with her? You lost her, you good-for-nothing shepherd! What have you done with Lody?"

"Berwyn!" Eldrast pulled his wife off Einur.

"I didn't do anything!" yelled Einur. "You had her, I tell you! That's why I didn't come back to you, 'cause you had her safe!"

"We did not!" screamed Berwyn, and began to weep. Eldrast pulled her into his arms and glanced at Einur, who raised his hands and shook his head.

"I know," mouthed Eldrast. He smoothed Berwyn's hair, and soon her weeping ended. Red eyes made a feeble attempt of smiling at Einur.

"I'm sorry," she whispered.

"It's okay."

"We can't enter the city," Eldrast stated. "They're watching it – for you, Einur."

"Why they're making such a to-do over a single escaped sacrifice, I will never know," murmured Berwyn.

Einur raised his eyebrows... he could've

explained it.

"No matter why the fuss. There's not a way in the world you could get into that city alive, Einur, and don't you try it."

"I don't need to as long as you can tell me where to find the sea fairies."

Berwyn cast a fleetingly frightened look at Eldrast, who returned it.

"Einur," began Berwyn, as Eldrast edged towards the young man. "You can't trust the sea fairies..." Eldrast was coming closer. "They're treacherous and false."

Eldrast darted sideways and captured both Einur's arms in his. Einur gave a cry and tried to wrench himself free, but the older man was too strong. He held the boy fast whilst Berwyn produced a rope and wound it about his wrists and ankles.

"Wha – "

His words were cut off by a strip of fabric which Eldrast whipped over his mouth. He then dragged Einur towards a dense copse of trees, where Berwyn secreted him with a thick layer of branches and leaves. He made a wild struggle to free himself as they slipped quietly away, but it was in vain – Berwyn's knots were true.

Fury was his only function for a good while, until it gave way to violent self-reproach. *Well, fool, you were right about them after all. Much good it'll do you now... and much good it'll do Lody. Stupid fool, to fall for their trick with your parents' names! Satisfied?*

Coenburg slipped out of Einur's knapsack and began to chatter excitedly. Einur twisted around, only to see the ferret run off.

He didn't even try to call him back.

Kemaý and his sister Brida were waiting beside a small seacraft. Kemaý's face was rugged from years spent at sea, his pale hair messy. His hand dwarfed Lody's when he took it to kiss as though she were a great lady, yet he took great care not to crush it. Brida was as tall in stature as her brother, though far more delicate, but in the way of features they might've been twins.

Whilst Kemaý had kissed Lody's hand, Brida hugged her tightly and whispered in her ear, "We'll find your brother pretty soon. When Vaal finds him, he'll bring him straight to the Island."

Lody gave a shy smile.

"How'd you like to cross Sarhadë now?"

Lody nodded until the blood rushed to her head. "I should like it very well, miss."

Haledon was laughing at her. "Climb in the boat, silly."

Kemaý stretched out a hand to her and she clambered over the side, followed by Brida. Haledon shoved the craft off the shore before boarding himself. Brida and Kemaý took up the oars and began to row.

"How long will it take?" enquired Lody.

"We'll be in the boat all night," said Brida. "I've made a snug little bed for you below the deck." She pointed, and Lody shot down the hatch to explore.

Footsteps sounded near Einur and he turned his head. Two figures stood above him, no more than silhouettes in the night's dark.

"Einur?" said one.

The voice was familiar but he couldn't recall where he'd heard it. He grunted, the only reply he could make through the gag. The other reached down, unsheathing a dagger, and cut the cloth from Einur's mouth.

"Wonder who did this."

"They're rascals," Einur said after working his jaw for a moment. "Calling themselves my friends and then turning on me."

"Well, they sure saved us some work," the first chuckled. "And Coenburg is one smart ferret. Glest, take his feet."

Between the two of them they lifted Einur, and he was carried through the trees into the city. They deposited him in a heap at the door of an old shack, then knocked. *Tap tap, bang, tap, bang.*

"Not locked," croaked someone within, and the man called Glest kicked it open. The voice swore. "If you break the Achielakf door..." A number of threats ensued. Glest merely laughed.

"Much ill you could do me. You're as tied up with sickness as this boy is with ropes."

"Ahhhhh." A sigh of satisfaction came from the corner. "You've brought him."

"That's right."

"Bring him here."

Glest's companion leaned down, unknotted the bonds from Einur's ankles, and propelled him towards the corner. An ancient hand reached out of the shadows, groping for the boy, and he recoiled. Glest's hand halted him and moved him inexorably forward again.

"Stay, boy. Give me your hand."

"I won't," muttered Einur.

Glest cackled with laughter. "He won't? He can't! He's all tied up!"

"Then untie him, stupid."

Sullenly Glest obeyed, slitting the ropes with his knife.

"Now give me your hand."

Glest seized Einur's wrist and shoved it towards the searching hand. A long sharp nail moved across the palm whilst Einur stood stock still, stoically trying to ignore it.

"We were right," the voice said at last. "Boy."

Einur refused to make the acknowledgement that was clearly expected.

"Boy." The tone remained cracked, but there was stone behind the veiling gentleness.

"What?"

"You could do much for us. Will you join us?"

"Are you joking? Do you take me for an idiot?"

"I take you for a boy who loves his sister." The speaker leaned forward and for the first time Einur saw his face: old and greatly wrinkled, yet very much alive. "We have Lody."

Nothing but his eyes showed his emotion. "That's a lie."

The hard black eyes held Einur's. "Is it?"

"If it's not, then prove it."

"She has been on Hornlë Island these past two days. You will come with us and see her." His eyes screwed themselves hypnotisingly into Einur's. "You will come with us."

Einur swayed. "I'll come with you."

His hand was dropped, there was a brief low sound, and he lost consciousness.

13

DO NOT LET ME SINK

A smirking face met Einur when he opened his eyes. Not Glest – the other one.

Scholar Elres.

"Believe the Most Illustrious now?"

Einur glanced about. "I don't see Lody."

"His power to send you here in but a second hasn't convinced you he could have your sister?"

"He *could* have her. Nothing's saying he *does* have her."

Elres stretched out a hand and yanked Einur to his feet. "Come."

He tripped along behind Elres' hurried pace until the man slowed.

"Look there."

Obediently Einur followed Elres' indicating arm to where Lody played on a beach, watched by a flaxen-haired girl and two young men. He writhed, trying to extricate his arm from Elres' grasp, but the scholar had been expecting that and detained him with a grip that was impossible to fight against.

"So?"

"Let... me... go," he threw back through clenched teeth.

"Oh, no. She's quite happy as she is. We'll just leave her be."

Einur made a tremendous effort, yanking his arms free. "Lody!" he yelled.

Elres downed him with a cruel kick to the knees. "Lody!" The four on the beach glanced up. "'Ware for Lody! Watch for the little girl! A murderous madman is attacking me!"

Einur struggled up and flew at him. He was atop the fake scholar in a moment, pummelling him mercilessly. "Liar!" he threw at Elres between punches. "Hateful... evil... liar!"

"Is that you, Elres?"

Running footfalls came near. Einur didn't bother to look; he bounced up and hightailed it across the field.

"It's the boy," gasped Elres, and the newcomer tore after Einur.

Years of living outdoors had conditioned Einur so that he could run for several miles without tiring, whilst Haledon had been raised in a high-ranking family and soon realised there was no way he could catch up with the boy.

"Einur! Stop, I'm your friend!"

Einur paused and looked back.

"Please – come back."

"You think I'm crazy?"

Haledon stepped forward, and Einur instantly did the opposite.

"Don't come any nearer."

"Will it change your mind to hear how much Lody wants to see you?"

Einur's face contorted. "How dare you let my sister's name come out of your filthy mouth?"

Haledon raised his hands in despair. "May I

at least bring your love to her?"

Exhaustion collapsed over Einur and all the tension in his body sagged away. "Yes."

Haledon nodded to him and turned around, returning to Elres. Einur watched him departing, too worn out to move. His legs softened, then folded under him.

"Hey you!"

His head flew up.

"Yes, you!"

Somehow he got once again to his feet and took off. Twice he glanced behind him; Elres was not far away. He closed his eyes and took a sobbing breath – and tripped over a root. *Get up.* The scholar was not thirty feet from him. *Run.* He stumbled forward.

Elres caught up with him.

And ran past.

Still shouting for him to stop.

Einur stared after him. *What in Kelyan?* But his mind refused to process anything. He sank to the ground.

Or was it a feather bed?

So soft.

"*Pe tiki lymf dana?*"

He tried to groan. *Am I never to be given rest?*

It was the most ethereal creature he'd ever seen, standing so lightly before him that it seemed it was hovering. There were drops of water in its coppery locks, locks crowned with a golden ribbon; its gown was pale green and left its arms bare. Beyond the creature... flowers, of every colour under the sun, ornamenting grass of the lightest green. The trees bowed over a brown creek that snaked silently between banks to whose very edge the flowers grew.

And it was speaking to him, in his own tongue now.

"I drew the veil. But for mortals it can only be drawn for a certain time. Come, now."

"I'm so tired," he whispered.

The creature reached out and touched Einur's forehead with one fingertip.

"That will last you until we reach my home. It is not far."

Energy filled his veins, and he felt himself following the creature, stepping as delicately as it did. Truly it wasn't far: almost before he knew it the creature was leading him to the sea's edge – and into the water, deeper and deeper. For only so long could he trust the creature. As the first wave caressed Einur's chin he stopped.

"It's too deep."

"You have been marked with the touch of a sea fairy. You shall not drown. Follow."

What can I do? He followed.

A wave broke over his head and he stumbled, choking on salt water.

"I told you I can't," he gurgled.

Again the fairy turned to him. "Trust."

It says it's a sea fairy. Maybe it's okay. He released his doubts and drew in a breath. Again he nearly choked, but this time it was with shock.

"I can breathe!" he exclaimed. "And I can talk underwater!"

The fairy smiled. "Now hurry. My mark will not last much longer."

He followed it a couple moments longer before it halted and waved its arm around. "The Sands of Lybroë. The realm of the sea fairies."

Just beyond Einur and the fairy, the water came to an abrupt end, forming a sort of wall.

High above their heads it arched up to create a roof so clear that the clouds in the sky were visible through it. Ahead, the Sands of Lybroë stretched out interminably. The fairy took Einur's hand and led him through the wall of water.

"Now we must find my king."

It skimmed across the Sands, but Einur could no longer do the same. As the fairy had warned, the effects of its touch had worn away, and he ran to keep up with it, only the newness of everything keeping him from collapsing.

"High King!" The fairy knelt briefly to an invisible creature.

"Nellothien – you have returned."

"High King, I have brought a mortal."

A second fairy materialised before Einur's eyes.

"Of which Tribe do you spring, son of land?"

"I... I... I am of the Third Tribe, High King."

"Indeed. I see that, at the least, you have not the evil thoughts of the First or Second. Son of land, how can it be that you are of the Third Tribe and yet come hither from the far land?"

A bolt shot through Einur's stomach. "I..."

"High King, I think he is not a spy," put in Nellothien, tremulously.

"Your thought is true. The mortal is no spy." The High King faced Einur and extended both arms, palms facing upwards. "Wilt accept the homage of Aldindir, High King of the Fairies of the Sea?"

Instinctively Einur placed his palms on those of the fairy King.

"I do accept it," he answered steadily.

"Thou, O King of the Third Tribe, art highest of all kings in the universe. Alone of the kings of earth hast stood firm against the evil that stretched its claws about our world."

"Do you not stand firm?"

"It is not a meritorious thing, O King, that the fairies have resisted, for the Master has created us as such that we do not turn to evil ways."

"High King, are my people here?"

Aldindir bowed his head. "They are here."

Tears sprang to Einur's eyes. "I've found them. I've found them."

"Nellothien."

Before the High King she curtsied.

"Find Afiawyr and bring him here to me."

She flew to do his bidding.

I've found them.

14
GIVE US A KING

Nellothien returned with Afiawyr in short order: a mortal man of good stature with long hair that seemed unsure whether its natural colour was blond or brown. His face was strong and his dark eyes steely yet kind.

He knelt to the High King.

"Afiawyr, you must meet Einur."

Afiawyr rose and nodded at Einur. "My pleasure, Einur."

"It will be more than your pleasure," stated Aldindir. "It shall be your joy."

Now Afiawyr was confused. His eyes

flicked back and forth between Einur and Aldindir. "How so, High King?"

"Einur is your distant kin – through your forefather Alaril."

Afiawyr's eyes glinted, and with his left hand he clenched the silver chain about his neck into his fist. His right hand he held out to Einur, but when the young man reached to take it he jerked it back. Instead he dropped to one knee.

"My sword is yours, my King."

"I thank you," replied Einur. Then he took Afiawyr by the arms and raised him, and embraced him.

"The Master bless you," said Afiawyr, breaking away. "The Master bless you, cousin."

A smile broke on Einur's lips. "And you, cousin."

"Nellothien."

"High King."

"Take the King and show him the room next mine." Aldindir swept his arm through the air and Einur watched as a large cottage appeared. "This is my palace, King Einur. We do not like our homes gaudy but in quiet taste."

"I'd rather live in a cottage than a castle, High King."

Beneath a pointed turret roof, an empty arch was the door into the seaweed-covered cottage. Nellothien shimmered down a bright passageway and paused before the room at its very end.

"The High King desires you would freshen yourself within, and rejoin him thereafter, if you would, King Einur."

"Thanks." Einur began to enter the chamber, but a sudden memory held him back. "How do you know that? He said no such thing."

"Indeed he did, great King, but not with words spoken."

"Oh."

It did not take Einur long to wash his face and hands with the water that sat in a silvery-blue basin at the far end of his room. He was at Aldindir's side before ten minutes passed.

"You wished, of course, to see your people, King Einur. Afiawyr has gone to gather them."

As the High King spoke the first trickle of people arrived; mostly men. However, they were quickly flooded by a crowd of women and children dressed in what must have been their very finest garments. They regarded Einur with obvious curiosity, especially the children, and even more especially one little girl in the front, hand tucked into her mother's. She looked just like Lody.

Einur swallowed hard.

Afiawyr appeared out of the mob and came to stand at Einur's side.

"Now has come Einur, son of Eldrast, son through many fathers of Eriand. I herald the return of our King!"

"All hail our King Einur!" Nearly the entire Third Tribe was cheering, excepting only a number of women who wept. The mother of the little girl was one of these, and Afiawyr stepped forward, put an arm around her, and brought her to Einur. She sank into the deepest curtsy.

"My King, may I have the presumption to introduce to you my wife Cavalia."

Einur raised Cavalia and kissed her on the cheek. She wiped her eyes and glanced around for her daughter. But Afiawyr already had the child by his side.

"And your daughter, cousin?"

"Esmel, my King, ten years old."

"She closely resembles my own sister." Einur bent down and gravely shook Esmel's hand. "Won't you greet me? You're my cousin too, you know."

She curtsied gravely, the image of her mother, bar Cavalia's tears. Then she dimpled impulsively and beckoned for him to lean down further.

"Does this mean the High King doesn't rule us anymore?" she whispered in his ear. "Will you make new laws?"

Make laws? Somehow such an idea had never entered Einur's head in the few moments he'd allowed himself to consider his kingship.

"I don't know," he whispered back. "Don't you like his laws?"

"He doesn't let us ever go up on the Island, and, you know, I should really like to see what it's like on land."

Of course... not one member of the Third Tribe could have set foot on land in five thousand years.

"I think you'll be able to go ashore someday,

though likely not for awhile."

Esmel laughed and danced away from him. "Mother! The King says I can go on the Island sometime!"

The look Cavalia turned on Einur was respectful, but annoyance was visible through the mask.

"We shall see, love," she told her daughter.

Afiawyr's face was darkened as he shepherded his family back into the crowd and re-emerged with three other men, whom he named to Einur. After this he wordlessly communicated with the High King, then spoke to Einur.

"King Einur, will you take a moment to speak with us?"

"Of course."

They moved a good distance away from the people, who relaxed and set up a symphony whose parts were made of quiet individual conversations.

"King Einur, can it be right to make false promises to our children?"

Einur's eyebrows crinkled. "False promises?"

"We cannot leave this haven without being leapt upon by our enemies. Please, do not give my daughter visions of a life on land."

Einur settled his weight onto his right side. "Firstly, cousin, can the Illyrië know you are here? And secondly, my purpose is to cause their downfall."

One of the men snorted quietly. Einur whirled to face him, and took a gamble on which name had been his. "Merim, have you objections to this?"

The laughter went out of his eyes. "No, my King. None."

"You think I cannot do this?" He turned to each of the others in turn. "You think I cannot do this?"

Afiawyr was the only one who met his eyes. "In all honesty, my King, I think it is a high and noble quest, but not to be accomplished."

"Can the Master of the Harmony not accomplish such a thing?"

"Where has the Master been these five thousand years?"

Did you not say that you trust me?

Einur turned on the one who spoke – he had

no recollection of this man's name. "On my council I will have men who trust in the Master and none else. Are you with me?"

The man nodded, flushing, followed in the gesture by the other two and Afiawyr.

"Very good." He swung slowly around on his heel, gazing into each pair of eyes in turn. "Yet furthermore I have been personally tasked with the downfall of our enemy."

No one spoke, although he could see the question hovering on their lips.

"By a man named Eigion."

Eyes widened; heads bobbed reverently. Einur's royal facade dropped. "You know Eigion?"

"And who of the faithful does not?" questioned Aldindir. "He is the Master's own herald."

Einur felt that he should have expressed some sort of surprise, but he couldn't. All the time, the connection had been clear as a cut diamond. "I see. He told me to find the Lost Tribe, and their King."

"What do you intend to do now that's done?"

"The second part of my mission was to figure out a sacrifice that has to be made. He didn't say what exactly it was."

"Can we go to war?"

Merim's question was directed not to Einur but to Afiawyr.

"If we must," he answered. "Our armoury is full – our smiths have had nothing else to do, my King."

"Shall we go to war? It is indeed a sacrifice."

This time Merim was addressing Einur.

I'm fifteen, he protested silently. *I shouldn't be making this kind of decision!*

You're a King, Einur Landman, a King of a great line.

Highest of all kings of the universe, Aldindir had said.

Help me, Master!

He exhaled deeply.

"We shall go to war."

15

THE KING WALKS AMONG YOU

Before anything else was done, Einur sat with his council to compose a challenge to the Illyrië. It took much time and Einur agonised over every detail, but finally Afiawyr brought him a text with which he was content to be satisfied.

To the Most Illustrious High Priest Sestimon of Kelyan (this was the part which Einur had most contested, but Afiawyr insisted that they at least employ the courtesy of using the man's official title), *King Einur Landman of the Third Tribe of Lo'Rien issues challenge of battle.*

For it is found that the Illyrië mock the glory of the Master in worshipping a false god, and that they commit atrocity against the people by sacrificing children to their god. King Einur will lead his armies from his refuge to the Island of Hornlë, where he shall await your reply, whether such be by herald or by the approach of your army.

Einur gave it a nod.

"How quickly can our messenger deliver this?"

"If he leaves early in the morning he can reach the mainland before dusk. From the shore it is not five hours' journey to the Salýd Woods and the Temple of Achiel. He will be there by midnight tomorrow."

"The *Great* Achiel," muttered Einur before he could check himself.

"What?" Afiawyr glanced at him sharply.

"My apologies – a fifteen years' habit is hard to break."

"Of course." Still, Afiawyr observed his cousin for a moment before dropping his gaze back to the parchment. "I will have a scribe write this out."

By the time Einur woke late in the morning,

the messenger was long gone, and the men of the Third Tribe were everywhere, cleaning weapons and armour. Einur himself was fitted with armour, something else he had not considered. They dressed him in a hauberk and leggings of mail; strapped vambraces over his heavy leather gloves. Over the hauberk they deposited a tunic of dull dark green, unadorned save for embroidery about the neck and bottom hem, and the sign of a fish handsomely emblazoned in gold across the chest.

The entire outfit felt wrong. *I wasn't cut out for this.*

Greatest king of all.

He clanked out of the armoury in his uncomfortable metal boots, glimpsing Afiawyr nearly immediately. The latter looked Einur over as he stood awkwardly, weight all on one side again, then released a chuckle.

"One can tell you've never worn armour before, cousin."

"Never even *seen* armour before," replied Einur, ineffectively working to keep his own smile in check.

"Nor yet a weapon, I suppose. I'll need to

remedy that, and quickly. Let me see that sword."

Einur tried to unsheathe it. Afiawyr snorted softly.

"With your right hand, cousin."

Einur raised his eyebrows, shrugged, and switched hands. Afiawyr stepped back from him and swung the sword in the air, tested its sharpness with his thumb.

"This one's the best we have, cousin."

The young king flushed. "Will you teach me how to use it?"

"No doubt. Come with me – we'll practise on the Sands."

Contrary to what he'd expected, Einur found that he picked up the basics rapidly and Afiawyr could soon move on to teaching him more complicated manoeuvres.

"There is no contesting your descent, cousin! Eriand had great skill with a blade, they say."

"You think I have skill?" Einur lunged at Afiawyr, who instinctively blocked him.

"Indeed!"

Their fighting was all for amusement now,

and when Einur finally tired, both were laughing. "Am I ready for battle, cousin?"

"You will not shame your people, my King."

Warmth glowed through Einur. "Tomorrow?"

"Tomorrow."

Einur retired early, but sleep only teased his eyelids. He pictured Lody, hustled off by that trio back on the Island. Was she still there, and if she was, would she be in danger during the battle? *I've no expectation the High Priest will refuse our challenge.*

Were her kidnappers hurting her at this very moment?

Peace, Einur.

"I'm afraid," he whispered into the dark.

I am with you. I am your strength. It is my sign your armour carries. Fear not, Einur.

"I'm only a fool of a peasant boy."

Fool? Perhaps. But my fool.

Einur fell asleep.

When Einur came to review his army, he was mildly surprised to find that Aldindir alone of the fairies was there. He turned a questioning look on the High King.

"Are your people not joining mine, High King?"

"No, King Einur. As we do not join in the sins of mortals, we do not join in their wars. This is your fight."

"I see." The light went out of Einur's eyes as he scanned the assembly. "How many men have I, Afiawyr?"

"Five hundred thousands, my King."

"And how many men do you calculate the Illyrië will have?"

"They have the entirety of Kelyan at their disposal, my King. They could have twice five hundred thousands."

"But the Island will not hold a million and a half men."

"No, my King."

"That is a small comfort."

Afiawyr let Einur stand silently for some time before touching his shoulder.

"We must go."

Einur started as though waking from a trance. "Thank you, Afiawyr. But – how shall we reach the Island? Can the fairies mark so many men?"

"I myself will touch you, King Einur," interrupted Aldindir, "and through you this power shall mark your people."

Einur bent his head and the fairy King briefly touched his forehead.

"May the Master keep you in his love and bring you safely back."

"I thank you, High King." He embraced Aldindir. Then he faced the army. "Now, shall we break the bondage in which we have been held for five thousand years?"

A mighty cheer broke from the men.

"The Master's favour be upon you," were Aldindir's final words as Einur turned from him to lead his army.

For all the men with the sole exception of Einur, it was a wholly new experience as they stepped out of the water and saw the bare sky for the first time in their lives. Undoubtedly the Sands of Lybroë were lovely, but land was the true home of the Third Tribe, and every leaf, every blade of grass, every colour of nature was outlined vividly to their eyes. Their first glimpse of land – and for many, surely their last.

"My King." Afiawyr tapped Einur on the arm. "You realise not one man among us knows the lie of this island."

Einur started. "Lody might."

"Pardon me?"

"My sister. This very moment she's held captive on this island. If we can find her, perhaps she can tell us how it sits."

"And how old is your sister, my King?"

"Ach, call me cousin, Afiawyr! Maybe I'm King, but I don't feel like it, and I hate such ceremony."

"Then cousin, how old is Lody?"

"Eight." He did a brief accounting with his fingers. "No. Nine as of yesterday."

"Forgive me, but I don't see how she could know what would be advantageous ground for us."

"Of course. I'd forgotten."

"Shall I send out scouts?"

"Yes, do that. But Afiawyr... come back to

me after you've done that."

"I will." Afiawyr bowed and retreated. Einur paced back and forth until his cousin returned.

"Afiawyr."

"Cousin?"

"You and I are going to find Lody. And we'll kill the ones who hold her."

Afiawyr laid a hand on Einur's shoulder. "Einur – I know what your feelings are. I myself have a daughter Lody's age! But have you actually pondered the possible consequences of doing such a rash act? If you are killed, Einur Landman, your people have no leader."

"Afiawyr, if I'm killed in battle, they have no leader! Lody's my heir, isn't she? If she too is murdered or secreted away by these kidnappers, then you are again without a ruler, and this time forever!" He took a breath to calm himself. "We go now."

After a second, Afiawyr dropped to one knee and bowed. "You have more strength than might immediately appear, my King."

16
THEY WERE LOYAL

The two of them pushed through bracken on their way to the northern tip of the Island. "If they know you saw them – which you say they do – they'd've headed as far away from their original area as they can," Afiawyr had explained. Einur recalling he'd originally seen Lody on the southwestern side, Afiawyr examined the map the sea fairies had provided, and traced a course northward from their own starting point.

Of a sudden Afiawyr flung out an arm before Einur.

"I heard something."

"I've heard a thousand things since we started."

"This noise wasn't a squirrel."

"No – it wasn't." Einur and Afiawyr spun round. "You remember me, eh?" laughed Haledon, observing the fury in Einur's eyes. "I guess you came to find me after all."

"Where's my sister?" Einur growled, taking a step forward.

The mirth went out of Haledon's eyes. "Of course. Follow me."

Afiawyr scowled. "You expect us to fall for that?"

"Yes."

"I'm going," muttered Einur to his cousin.

Afiawyr shrugged and trailed after them.

Out of nowhere a little girl leapt onto Einur. "Einur, Einur, Einur!" she shrieked. And Einur burst into tears.

"Are you okay, Lody?" he asked when he'd calmed.

"Haledon's taken awful good care of me," she said seriously, glancing over Einur's shoulder at that young man. "And Brida. Brida is Kemaÿ's sister."

"None of them has hurt you?"

"Of course not! They were just keeping me safe whilst Vaal went to find you."

"Vaal?"

"I didn't like him, and – " she bent to whisper in his ear – "Haledon doesn't either. He didn't tell me that but I can see."

Einur freed himself from Lody's grasp and faced Haledon with a look that might've killed.

"What Lody says is true. Vaal's my childhood friend, but he got in with bad company a few years ago. I'm ashamed to say I didn't realise just how rotten he'd grown till recently, so I stuck with him. A few months ago I got sick of it and tried to bow out, but he threatened to have my sister and her family murdered. So I did what I could to sabotage him from inside. And now my sister's safe away and Lody's with you, and I wondered... could I go with you and fight for your King?"

Afiawyr grinned. "Whyever not?" He winked at Einur. "You think?"

"Afiawyr! Hush!" Einur was staring eastward. Afiawyr listened for three seconds.

"Back to the camp – now!"

"Wait." Haledon caught Afiawyr's arm. "What about my friend and his sister?"

"You go with Lody, Afiawyr, I'll wait with Haledon."

"No, Einur, if anyone goes now it's you. Take your sister and run, we'll catch up with you. Don't argue!"

Einur stared at him.

"Please."

Einur took Lody's hand and they started down the pathway. Looking back, Einur saw his cousin and Haledon duck into the trees. Afiawyr caught sight of him and gave him a nod with a smile, but Einur saw the look he hid and it horrified him: Afiawyr was the man of war, the fearless one, the one who knew what to do... *isn't he?*

Lody tugged on him and he bent to kiss her hair in reassurance, and she skipped on ahead of him. "Am I going to see soldiers?" she asked, missing the dark veil that drew over the sun.

Einur did not miss it.

Gernhr gave the Prelisër Commander yet another glare behind his back as he unbuckled his sword and threw it down before him, catching a sympathetic grin from his father, Cednhr.

"It's wretched and stupid," Gernhr muttered.

The Prelisër spun round; his sharp eyes seemed to read all Gernhr's hateful and rebellious thoughts. "Did you speak?"

Gernhr lifted his hands, let his mouth drop open in a fool's expression.

The Prelisër moved closer. "You're not an idiot, Gernhr Smith, and neither am I. I've been High Priest in Ledmi since before your mother birthed you."

The young man smiled the most vacuous smile he could muster and raised his hands again.

Eyes narrowed, the Prelisër hissed, "Watch yourself. Watch yourself yet more carefully that I will watch you, and you may return home when this is done."

Gernhr dropped his pose and stared straight into the Prelisër's eyes. Their gazes wrested against each other's until the Prelisër laughed grimly.

"Watch yourself, Gernhr Smith."

Cednhr set his hand on his son's shoulder as the Prelisër Commander strode away. "Careful, son – always avoid the Prelisër."

"I'm telling you, dad, I'm *never* fighting with them. *Never* fighting against Einur."

"Son, that boy's a month younger than you and a shepherd. I'll believe he's a king when I see him wearing a crown."

"Well, you might just get to, dad." He took hold of Cednhr's arms. "Dad, come with me when I get out of here tonight."

"You must be the red-socked ferret, Gernhr! Thinking you could get away from this camp!"

"Dad, I told you. I'm not fighting for the Illyrië and if I stay I'll end up doing just that – or being killed for treason to the Illyrië and the Prelisër Most Illustrious Field Marshal." He snorted. "Or in talk a body can understand, the High Priest of Kelyan."

"Gernhr... I share your hatred for their ways... but that's no excuse for disrespecting the Most Illustrious."

"Are you laughing last on me, dad? He kills children and I can't disrespect him?"

Cednhr shrugged slowly. "Go. But I can't come with you – I wouldn't make it, and I won't risk you failing just 'cause I'm no good at sneaking."

"Dad..."

"No, son." He embraced Gernhr. "Go carefully."

Gernhr's expression broke. "Blessings on you, dad. I'll see you after all this is done."

A smile reached his father's eyes. "I love you, Gernhr."

"I love you, dad."

He waved his hand in farewell, glanced around for the Prelisër, and slipped away into the night.

"My lord?" A soldier peered through the flap of Einur's tent. "A fellow's here... a rough boy, says he must see you. He won't go away."

"Let him come in then."

"I beg your pardon, my lord, but in that case might I stay with you? Like as not he's some murdering slave of those devils'."

"Language, Latkim! Give them some respect with your words."

"Sorry, my lord. It's easy to forget. But like I was saying, my lord, may I stay to guard you?"

Einur inclined his head. "Thank you, Latkim. You may stay."

Latkim bowed out of the tent, momentarily returning with the visitor. Einur rose to receive him, and for a few seconds the two young men stood still.

"...Gernhr?"

Then he ran forward and the friends embraced each other.

"I've missed you, Gernhr!"

"And I you, Einur!" Suddenly Gernhr blanched and jumped away. "I forgot..." He took in Einur, his rich light blue tunic, embossed brown shirt, vambraces strapped to his arms, gold circlet around his blond waves. "...You look like a king."

Einur gave an awkward laugh, voice breaking into a squeak at its end. "I guess I do."

A sly smirk crept across Gernhr's lips. "Alanara back home would love to see you now."

"I look that good?"

Both boys broke into laughter, thinking of the girl who'd had a crush on Einur forever. Einur's laugh died abruptly, however, as he thought of how far away home and Alanara were – and how likely it was they'd never meet again. Gernhr read his mind and quieted as well. After a pause Einur turned to Latkim.

"You may go, Latkim – this is an old friend of mine and no danger."

The soldier bowed and scuffed his foot, backed out of the tent.

"You even have a guard!" teased Gernhr.

"Not officially," returned Einur. "He thought you likely to kill me."

Gernhr turned serious. "They love you, Einur."

"What?"

"Your men love you. I could tell it just walking through your camp and talking to them."

Tears wormed past Einur's defenses. "I never thought... Well, but where did you come from?"

"They were conscripting, the Illyrië were. So naturally me and my dad got picked up. I wasn't standing for it, though, 'specially as the enemy was my best friend, so I got out."

"And your dad?"

Gernhr's lip, formerly a hallmark of manly firmness, quivered. "He stayed, didn't think he'd make it out without getting caught."

"He'll be okay, Gernhr."

"Yeah." He sniffed.

"Much as I would enjoy continuing our conversation, I think it wise to take rest now," stated Einur, shoulders squaring of their own accord. "Much will happen on the morrow."

Gernhr grinned weakly. "You just went into King style."

Colour attacked Einur's cheeks. "Sorry."

"But you're right. Where'm I sleeping?"

"To be honest, I really do not know. But wait, I'll entrust you to Latkim. He can show you how things work. In fact, he probably knows such details better than I." He called out to the soldier, who popped in immediately, evidently having still kept guard over the king. "Please, Latkim, will you take care of Gernhr?"

"Of course, my lord."

"My lord, eh?" Gernhr raised his eyebrows with a smirk.

Einur dreamed he was walking in the clouds. Or rather, not walking but floating, floating on the breast of the wind. The air was alive with gentle voices, but their words were unintelligible. Stay – one voice he could understand.

"There is no greater love than this, Einur Landman."

"No love greater than what?" he asked silently.

"Greater love than this has no man, Einur Landman, that he lay down his life for his friends."

His dream faded and Einur fell yet more deeply asleep.

17
FLEE FROM EVIL

Afiawyr and Haledon waited long for Brida and Kemaý as the sun moved westwards. Fifteen minutes turned into twenty, and twenty into a half hour before Afiawyr stirred from his easy position on the moss.

"I don't think they're coming, Haledon. We might as well go."

Haledon nodded wearily and they turned in the direction of the camp of the Third Tribe.

Little more than half a mile from where Haledon and Afiawyr had waited, the sole of Kemaý's already well-worn boot finally broke off, and he and his sister stopped to lash it back on. Bending over Kemaý's foot, they failed to observe that a second couple had approached and stood watching them from the protecting shelter of the trees. As they straightened, the taller of the newcomers stepped out.

"My greetings to you, stranger."

Out of habit and instinct Kemaý's hand rested on the hilt of his sword before the man's second word was finished. "Would you be friends of those who oppress?"

"Being the Illyrië?"

"Mine was the first question. Let yours be the first answer."

"Assuming that you do mean the Illyrië, no. We have spent years in undermining their power."

Kemaý loosed his hold on his sword and reached out to greet the stranger. "Welcome to you, then. We are in good company, Brida. Sir, I'm called Kemaý, and Brida is my sister."

"My wife is Berwyn, and I am Eldrast. Kemaý, Brida, have you by chance seen a young man – light-haired, medium height?"

"Seems to fit the description of our little

charge's brother, no, Kemaý?"

"Would his name have been Einur?" asked Kemaý.

Every trace of friendliness vanished instantly from both Eldrast's and Berwyn's manners. "What have you to do with Einur and Lody?" Eldrast snarled.

"We were taking care of Lody for our friend Haledon whilst he searched for Einur. Einur's somewhere on this island or very nearby."

Berwyn's shoulders sagged. "I guess I knew he'd found them when we got the news... but still, I'd hoped it was a coincidence."

"What news?" asked Kemaý.

"The Third Tribe sent a challenge of war to the Illyrië's high priest. In Putae they were saying it was issued by the Tribe's king, returned after five thousand years. That'd be why we came – if the King is with the Third Tribe, then so is Einur Landman."

"Maybe if we catch up to Haledon and Lody, we can find Einur together. The two of them can't be far ahead. In fact, we were just behind them a while ago, though they've likely gotten a head on us now we've stopped."

"Right, Brida!" Kemaý raised his eyebrows at Eldrast. "Will you come with us?"

"Anything to find Einur and Lody."

Twilight teased the path through the leaves as they passed the spot where Haledon and Afiawyr had waited, and it was pure chance that, as they passed, Brida noticed the parchment tacked to the tree trunk. She plucked it and scanned the few words scrawled on it.

The others halted as she called out, and Eldrast asked, "What does it say?"

Brida flushed and held it towards him. "I can't read."

"No shame," he replied as he took the parchment. "'Southward along the shore.' No difficulties in that."

They followed the trail as it took a downward slant, walking silently save for the occasional muffled curse when Kemaý stumbled over one of the abundant tree roots. Ahead of them now was an abrupt slope leading up again: a miserable prospect, for they were already tired and perhaps a little afraid of what might be found at the crest.

Eldrast at least had this thought, for he

turned to whisper instructions. "Single file, please – Kemaý, be our rearguard? Keep a ways back from the person before you; if one is captured perhaps the rest can escape."

They crested the hill, but even squinting into the night they could make out no enemies. "Are there wild animals on the Island?" Berwyn murmured to Eldrast as the four huddled.

"No. It's humans we watch for. Seems safe enough, though. Eh, Kemaý? You look a fighting man."

"I hear nothing," replied Kemaý. "Let's go on. No true safety till we've reached camp."

The way down was surprisingly steep, and it was a slow progress: leaning backwards to hold balance, one foot cautiously before the other, step after step. Only Kemaý, used to following multiple thoughts at once in such situations, still kept his guard when they reached the hill's foot. All yet seemed clear, but as Brida followed after Eldrast and Berwyn, Kemaý snatched at her arm and drew her back.

"There was a sound," he breathed in her ear.

Berwyn's cry cracked the night's silence, and within the space of two seconds, Kemaý...

...would have whipped out his dagger, had his arm not been pinned behind him, another man's hand firmly covering his mouth. Kemaý twisted in a move his years as a warrior had perfected, but the strength in his captor's arm was that of a blacksmith. He attempted another tactic: he let the weight drop from his body, going limp. Not entirely on guard, the man nearly lost his hold on Kemaý, but not quite.

A voice came from the dark. "How many have we, besides mine?"

Three voices replied, including that of Kemaý's captor.

"Get them back to camp, then."

They tramped through the unbroken woods, going opposite the directions in the note – north, on a slight slant towards the east. Trees dragged by, glimpsed only vaguely by Kemaý as he grew woozy from the force of his guard's grip. *Gotta keep alert*, he thought, and tried to count the trees he was dragged past. *Eleven... fifteen... twenty-one* – The woods came to an abrupt end and before the eight of them appeared, as though from nowhere, a vast encampment. A sentinel stepped from a tent as they approached, and demanded the password.

"The Great Achiel is lord," growled one of the Illyrië's men as the prisoners were hustled by. *Cleverly chosen,* Kemaý thought, *Haledon's friends probably wouldn't say that even to sneak into the camp.*

The captives were bound together and left in a guarded tent, and even determined as he was to remain awake, some force persuaded Kemaý's eyelids downward and would not allow them to open.

Oh, it was beautiful to sleep…

…stupid voices, invading peaceful rest…

"I recognised you the moment we got into the light of the camp."

I hate whispering voices, I'd almost rather he would talk aloud…

"I couldn't believe my eyes – has it been six years? – but here you tell me it's true… I pretended to be the change of watch to get to you. We can't have much time before they figure out what happened, so we've got to get out now."

…cruel hands, shaking him from slumber…

"Kemaý. Kemaý, are you okay? Kemaý?"

It's only Brida.

He sat up, shaking his already wild hair into a yet more knotted mane. "Yeah."

"We're escaping – leaving now."

They slunk along the sides of tents till they reached the camp's edge, whereupon their rescuer led them in a dart across a couple tens of feet into the safety of the forest.

Away from the Illyrië camp, the fogginess was dissipating from his brain and he could think clearly once more. The stranger – he was Kemaý's captor, and if his brawn told any tale, he was indeed the blacksmith Kemaý had thought him. Out of his element in the woods, he was glancing about, markedly unsure of himself.

"Do you know where we go from here?"

Eldrast was nodding, Kemaý could make it out in the faint light of the newly-risen moon. He was leader again, Berwyn's hand in his at the head of the little group. The other man walked just behind them, and Kemaý and Brida trailed after them as they talked quietly amongst themselves: the blacksmith seemed to be an old friend of Eldrast and Berwyn's. Kemaý caught close on nothing of their conversation but for the occasional mention of some mountain town and the stranger's name. Cednhr.

Presently Cednhr's voice raised furiously. "You *bound and abandoned* him?"

Berwyn's reply was heavily emotional. "You think we wanted to? It was for his good – it was to prevent something like this very war!"

"And what did it avail in the end?"

A miserable, mouse-like sound escaped Berwyn's lips and she huddled into Eldrast's shoulder. Eldrast turned to frown at Cednhr. "Ask your wife about it someday, she could tell you how such a love runs."

All went unspeaking until, with the morning's dawning, they came in sight of a second camp, far smaller than that of the Illyrië. They were confronted by a guard, hardly older than Einur yet with such an ancient look in his brown eyes. "Password!" he snapped – must have been his first time actually having to ask.

"We don't know it," Eldrast said quietly.

"Then I can't let you by," replied the young

man, dropping his hand unobtrusively to the sword which hung at his side.

"I understand you can't disobey orders, son... but somehow we must see King Einur."

"Not without you give the password." His fingers slipped about the hilts of his sword and tightened.

From the moment of Einur's waking, there was no spare moment. His men ate a meagre breakfast as the sun broke swiftly over the western horizon. Meal completed, they dispersed to arm themselves. At but the third hour from dawn, the army of the Third Tribe waited in readiness as their enemies gathered on the opposite side of the field.

Gernhr found his way to Einur and stood next him. Einur smiled.

"What?"

"Good luck, my friend," he muttered.

"And to you."

They rested, silent. Presently Gernhr stirred.

"Do you hear it, Einur?"

"A fell voice – there is a fell voice in the wind. As though someone were cooking up a sorcery."

"It may well be so." Einur bowed his head. "May the Master protect us."

Gernhr glanced sharply into his face. "You call on the Master as though it were the most natural thing in the world."

Einur was surprised. "But of course it is!"

"Wasn't so long ago it was the Great – Achiel – you called to for help."

A joyful realisation struck Einur. "Do you know, Gernhr, this is the first time I haven't actually had to correct myself praying to Achiel? At least not talking with someone like you. With the sea fairies and my Tribe it's different, easier to remember... but I'm talking to you and I remembered."

Gernhr set his hand on his friend's shoulder. "I wish I'd been with you the whole time. Now you've reached here and I'm still just starting."

"Have patience, and..." Eigion's words, now so familiar to Einur, came back to him. "And trust. Always trust."

Afiawyr, on Einur's right, interrupted to

swat Einur on the arm. "Look up."

Just as Einur did so, a dragon swooshed over their heads, flying nearly low enough to claw them.

"Watch out!" screamed Einur.

The entire army ducked just as two thunders – a full twenty – of dragons roared overhead. Their legs strained downward, snatching up men and letting them fall as they wheeled back to their masters. A tremendous fury flooded through Einur's blood as he watched his people die. How could anything be worth such a price? The Illyrië must fall, but how could anything be worth such a price?

"Archers, fire at will!"

A whine of arrows filled his ears, peppering the dragons with their sting as the beasts returned. Two fell; the men of the Third Tribe scattered as the mammoth bodies thudded onto the ground. The survivors retreated to attack again.

Einur's eyes fastened on the one that flew directly at him. He could see its eyes from where he stood... coal-black. *Efrix. I still kinda miss my dragon, even if they're nothing but evil. Even if he tried to get me killed.* He couldn't take his eyes from the creature. It flew closer and he could feel its fetid breath burning his nostrils.

"*Einur!*" Gernhr barrelled into Einur, knocking him flat. The dragon shrieked at its lost prey as it swooped past. Einur stood and dusted himself off. Screams erupted behind him and he closed his eyes momentarily, fighting back tears of horror and fury.

He gradually became aware of Afiawyr calling his name. "Einur – we've got to attack sometime. We'll only keep losing men."

Einur nodded. "Give the order." He drew his sword. Gernhr was watching him, and Einur grasped his hand. "The Master give strength unto your hand, Gernhr Smith."

Gernhr swallowed. "And to yours, Einur Landman."

Afiawyr's order resounded in his ears, and he was caught up in the charge.

18

TAKE UP YOUR CROSS

In the hours after the battle, Einur could not have told you what deeds he had done, for his memory of them was blacked out by the terrible thing that came to the Third Tribe of Lo'Rien.

It began as but a wisp of green mist that played about their ankles, and it grew to a cloud and blinded their vision, and it filled their lungs with poison. Many men fell then with no mark on their flesh. Who knows how that day might have ended, had not King Einur prayed in that moment to the Master of the Harmony, that their eyes might see and their lungs breathe. And then his mind cleared, and those of his men, and the king gave the order for retreat.

In his dream Einur found himself once more walking on the clouds, and now when the voice spoke to him, he sensed that the owners of all the other voices watched him.

"Greater love than this has no man, that he lay down his life for his friends."

In the morning his cheeks were salty from many tears.

He slid from his bed and washed his face of the tears. As he did so, Lody pattered into his tent and greeted him with a bright "Good morning!" He lifted his head dripping from the water and groped for a towel. *Already she has recovered from everything that has happened to her*, he thought as he embraced her, a twinge of jealousy at her resilience jolting through him. *Whilst I... I...*

"My lord – " Latkim paused when he saw Lody. Einur gently disengaged the child and rose from his knees. "My lord, a herald from the

Illyrië asks to see you."

And I am so heart-weary already. "I will see him."

The herald strode in after Latkim: a cocky fellow he was, with a self-confident smirk upon his features that irked Einur to his depths.

"My lord." The herald greeted him with a perfunctory bow, a nod of the head rather than the profound bow from the waist which a king merited. *You're at least fifteen years younger than me,* Einur felt he was thinking, *I shall not respect you.* "I bring you a challenge from my lord the Prelisër Most Illustrious Field Marshal, Sestimon High Priest of Kelyan."

"I am listening," said Einur, wishing Lody was not present.

"The Most Illustrious Sestimon High Priest of Kelyan sends unto Einur Landman King of the Third Tribe of Lo'Rien his greetings, and challenges him to face alone the Spirit of the Great Achiel, in whom King Einur professes not to believe. This challenge bring I, Esegar Faulkner of Anglesea, to King Einur from the Most Illustrious."

He finished his monotonous delivery with a grin directed at Einur. Einur stared in return. Esegar flinched and backed away a step or two.

"Your answer, sire?" He was sullen now.

How am I yet breathing? Einur felt as though he were stifling. He had to look away from Esegar; his eyes dropped to Lody. Her own eyes were like those of a doe, large and frightened, returning his gaze. *How can I give an answer before her? For surely I must accept, and I cannot do such a thing before her.*

He faced Esegar with a countenance that might have crumbled stone. Certainly it crushed the remains of the man's cockiness. "Tell Sestimon: Surely this is a great challenge and not one to be taken lightly, neither accepted nor refused upon the basis of one moment's consideration. At three hours past the midday meal, tell Sestimon, I shall send a herald with my reply."

Esegar slunk out in Latkim's wake. He would bring tales to the camp of the Illyrië of the boy-king whose heart and mettle were nothing like those of a boy.

Einur thought long. Then he went out alone

to walk in the forest.

Casting all thoughts of the Illyrië and war from his mind, he padded through the thick moss masking the soil. He pretended he was home again, exploring the mountainsides with Efrix close behind him. Many times they had done so, walking in contented silence through woods and meadows – often to their favourite spot, an outcrop of rock matted with moss even thicker than the moss in this forest. Ledmi was Einur's world then, but from high in the sky halfway up a mountain, it was merely a dark smudge in a much greater painting that was the Emeril Holding.

And now half of Western Kelyan, plus miles of salt water, lay between him and Ledmi far away.

He thought of his darling Lody who'd only ever had him; she barely knew how to mother her own doll, for she had no mother but Gernhr's. All this time, he'd been fighting for the triumph of good over evil, yes, but above all other motives rode his Lody. Nothing, *nothing*, was worth more to him than she was.

Not his very life mattered if she was safe.

"Have I your leave to intrude, lord?"

Einur wiped the tears away before rising from his knees. She was majestically built, tall and large, draped in deep vivid green with a river of obsidian tumbling to her waist.

"You were weeping," she said bluntly, hazel eyes hunting in his.

"I can't leave Lody all alone," he whispered.

"The war will make orphans of us all. Yet – Lody need not be one of them." Her eyes dug deeper into his soul. "You have a good heart, O King. I would give you the Emerald of Life. For Lody's sake."

"The Emerald of Life?"

"Whilst you hold this stone in your keeping, you cannot die. You could do what you must, yet return to Lody also."

She raised her hand, and in it was a great and beautiful gem, lit from within as though it burned. Unconsciously his hand stretched out towards it.

"I will gift it unto you, King Einur, that you may save your people and live."

"Lody," he replied, his eyes on the Emerald of Life.

"That you may save Lody and live for her."

His shuddering hand reached a little further and took the stone.

"For Lody."

He left her there without a farewell, striding homewards. Lody met him at the edge of the camp, and he bent and embraced her. "I love you," he murmured.

"I love you too. I missed you, Einur!"

"And I missed you." He put her back from him and looked directly into her eyes. "Now and forever, I'll always be with you, Lody. You hold my oath."

The night was not young when Einur found his bed. His herald whom he had sent to accept Sestimon's challenge had returned late, bringing with him instructions to meet the spirit upon the battlefield at the third hour from dawn's breaking. Only two others might accompany him, and he might carry a single weapon.

A third time he dreamed of the voices above the clouds. A third time he heard the words that haunted him.

"Greater love than this has no man, Einur Landman, that he lay down his life for his friends."

Even so his sleep was deep.

Einur woke at dawn and sent for Latkim to arm him. Neither spoke; Latkim only bowed as he backed from the king's tent. With Latkim's departure came Afiawyr and Gernhr just as Einur slipped the Emerald into a pouch about his neck. He could not speak of the stone to his cousin and friend, not even to drive the sorrow from their eyes. There was a commotion at the guard's post as they passed out of the camp, but Einur was oblivious to the woman's despairing cries and the man's shouts.

Before they reached the field already the green mist snaked about their feet, and a wall of it blurred their vision at the edge of the trees. Stoically they marched through it, defying it to poison their breath.

Oh, but it was a horror that met them on the other side, a horror of darkness that befouled the very life of their souls. Faithful Gernhr and valorous Afiawyr fell back in abhorrence of its ethos; only Einur thought of Lody and faced it unflinching.

"You desired to devour my sister," he stated. "Never shall you touch her, nor another mortal child. First would I die."

The figure within the cloud opened its mouth and sucked into itself all the mist that seeped around the two. Then it exhaled, the poison twisting towards Einur.

"In the name of the Master I banish you from this place!" he cried.

The mist dissipated and a piercing wail echoed and re-echoed from the figure's mouth. Einur stood down and gazed upon its shrinking terror. The breeze lifted and flung it away into nothing, and Einur swayed and fell.

Afiawyr sprang to raise him and cupped his hand to his cousin's cheek. It was flaming hot but it cooled under Afiawyr's hand. Einur's staring eyes refocused on Afiawyr and he tried to stand. Afiawyr got up with him.

"Cousin... you are weak. Sit and rest."

Einur shook his head. "There is no time. We

must bring the news back to the Tribe."

Gently Afiawyr pushed him back to the ground. "I will go." He allowed no debate, his strides taking him hastily out of sight amongst the trees.

Einur rose as though to follow him. "I'll rest easier alone in the woods. I must think."

He was keenly aware of Gernhr's eyes observing him, yet Gernhr merely said, "Be on your guard. When you return we can talk?"

"Of course."

He stepped into the forest and at once peace embraced him. Turning his face upwards, he stretched his arms wide and absorbed the silence. Leaves rustled and he whipped around to recognise Eigion. The old man's expression held no kindness.

"Give me the Emerald of Life."

"Why should I?" snapped Einur, inexplicably defensive. "The woman gave it to me."

"Three times you dreamed a dream, and still you accepted such a gift. Einur, you were foolish, foolish."

"Foolish?" he cried. "Foolish, to want to save my sister and stay with her?"

Eigion made no reply, his eyes attacking Einur – or so it seemed to Einur. He broke down. "I only wanted to protect Lody."

If he had expected Eigion to soften, he was not rewarded. "You told yourself that, and indeed it is true, but was there not pride laced into your decision? Did you not think that you could be the great king who defeated death?"

Always Eigion's words had commanded an answer from Einur. He gave a tiny nod.

"It is not your task to defeat death but another's who is to come." Einur looked up and Eigion's sternness evaporated. "With your contrition comes forgiveness. Now, take out the Emerald."

Einur reached into his pouch and drew out the Emerald. There was flame still in its core, and as Eigion touched it the fire sprouted about the sphere. Einur gasped, but Eigion did not flinch.

"There is no heat."

Hesitantly, Einur stretched out a finger and touched its tip to the Emerald. It was completely cool. "Is it sorcery?" he breathed, disgusted yet intrigued.

Eigion inclined his head without reply, buried deep in his own thoughts. The young king stood silent, gaze never leaving the old man. Finally he looked up.

"Once before you destroyed an evil thing at my bidding. Will you do so again?"

"Anything."

Eigion held out the Emerald and Einur understood. He drew his sword, set the gem on the ground, and smashed it with the hilts.

"Now return to your friend and spend with him what time you may."

His heart much lighter, Einur smiled. "The Master's blessings on you, my lord."

Eigion levelled an inscrutable gaze on Einur. "I will see you again, soon."

Einur cocked his head questioningly, but no answer came and he turned back to find Gernhr, whom he found waiting for him.

"You okay?"

"Yeah."

"That pouch you were wearing is gone."

"It was nothing important... Please, tell me what has happened to you since I left."

Einur sat and Gernhr dropped beside him,

gathering his thoughts. "It was three? – yes, three weeks ago. I'm guessing they anticipated your challenge, because it was right after Lody got away from them that they started the conscription. Speaking of that, you have to tell me how you and she were rescued."

"I will, but your tale first."

"Well, I was all for trying to get out of it, but dad convinced me it was safer not to refuse, and if I had to try escaping I should do it when no one would notice me amongst everyone else. Once all the men of Ledmi were collected we went around through Mourvh and collected their men too, then marched on down to Iloaar. Oh, and the innkeeper there said to give you greetings. I thought of asking if you'd been there and she told me about your stay at the inn. She said you got a ferret from one of her patrons. Do you still have it? I want to see a ferret."

"Sorry. It got away." Einur was staring off into the distance, a sudden chill latching onto his soul.

"Too bad. Anyway. After a couple days in Iloaar we went on to Anglesea. I was almost glad I'd gone. It was quite something to see the whole world. That's what it felt like anyway. But once we got here I thought it was about time to make my escape." He paused. "That's about all. What about your own escape?"

Einur did not reply and stood up abruptly.

"Is something wrong?"

A vague dark shape wisped across the field, low against the grass.

"Einur?"

He knew what he must do.

One step, another step, one more... And Gernhr realised what he was about.

So it was a race, and Gernhr had always won their races. But *I'll beat you someday*, Einur had promised once, and it was now that he fulfilled his promise. Kingly he appeared, standing there as the spirit of Achiel towered above him in the form of a dragon. Not a word either of them spoke, but the dragon belched forth his mist. And about Einur burst a shield of brilliant light that held off the mist that sought to penetrate it.

Einur drew his sword and raised it high. Tentatively the shield bulged outwards, and then it broke. The head of the dragon darted downwards and its jaws fell upon Einur. Mist swirled about them and both were hidden from view.

One thought alone filled his heart. *Lody.*

And then it was not the fabled blackness of death that met his eyes, but light, great glory and splendour more wonderful than anything on mortal earth. And he knew the voice that spoke out of the light.

"Well done, my good and faithful servant."

The clouds parted and a single ray of light dropped from the heavens and pierced the dragon, and all signs of the spirit and the mist were gone.

And Einur lay alone upon the grass.

19

PIECE THE FRAGMENTS

*T*o the great and lovely Queen of the Third Tribe of Lo'Rien, Aloden Landman, on the Isle of Hornlë, this second day of the eleventh month of the first year of the Freeing.

Don't listen to me, I'm just being an idiot.

Dearest Lody,

Maybe I should've written sooner. No, of course I should've written sooner. It is no excuse for me but replacing the whole way we were living in Ledmi is a lot of work. I've taken over the smithy work for my dad. You can see him getting older and tired, and he's gotten real busy with the village matters and everything. Everyone still thinks I'm too young to help with that, so I convinced dad to pass on the smithy to me instead. You probably wouldn't recognise me. With all the heavy work I'm getting very big and kind of dirty.

I'm sure the Third Tribe will be interested to hear how the First and Second are faring, so I'll explain how things are working in Ledmi. The Temple's torn down. We had a celebration that day. All of us came out with hammers and we beat it down, every stone. I never saw such a party. The festivals on the Middle Days didn't even come close. Dancing, singing, and feasting, and I won't pretend I didn't dance enough with Kania (you remember, she used to watch you sometimes for Einur). When things are figured out we're going to build a tabernacle in praise of the Master. Quite a few towns are doing that. No one seems to know what's happened to the Illyrië. They've simply disappeared.

The men voted on the matter and it's decided that Ledmi will have a chief from now on, elected by vote from amongst the townsmen every fifth year. Our first election is in a fortnight. Don't tell anyone, but I have a feeling they might choose my dad.

I think Einur would've been delighted to see what's happened. Look, Lody, maybe you already knew this but *he did it for you. Everything. He knew he was saving thousands of children but in the end every choice he made was about you. He died for the world but he died for you.*

Lody... I'm so sorry I ran off. I'm the greatest coward Kelyan ever knew. I know I should've stayed and told you all the whole story. I was glad I was in too much shock to tell more than I did – how the spirit came back and he faced it down and died. I woke up in the night and thought of telling you the horror of it and I was a baby, I knew I couldn't face you. So I ran. This letter, a year later, is me trying to be a bit less of a coward, although if I really had any courage I'd tell it to your face.

Oh Lody, I can't tell it at all.

I worked in the smithy for a while and that always helps so I'll try again.

We were talking and I was recounting my time with the Illyrië's army but soon I saw he was distracted. Next thing I knew he was gone, running across the field to where that awful mist had come back. Lody, we'd thought it was dead, the spirit was dead. It'd disappeared when he fought it before. Why couldn't I win the stupid race? I always won our races before! He got there first and I couldn't move. I was stuck where I was and I couldn't look away. I lost the race and I lost my best friend. I lost your brother and it was my fault.

That's why I can't face you.

From the hand of Aloden Queen of the Third Tribe to Gernhr, worthy smith of Ledmi. This being the seventeenth day of the fourth month of the second year of the Freeing.

My chief lady-in-waiting who is also my tutor and also my cousin Cavalia tells me a queen should address all her letters so. I think it is silly to address a friend in such fashion. Therefore I say rather, Dear Gernhr, it was perfectly lovely to receive a letter from you! I miss you a great deal although I have many friends here. Haledon has stayed with us, as have Kemaý and Brida, if you remember them. Kemaý married a girl from the Tribe two months ago and he is one of the greatest warriors in my army (which I do not think it should be called my army because I am only ten) but of course he has nothing to do since the Illyrië are disappeared into nothing!

I might say I am friends with Cavalia but she is my tutor as I said and very strict with me. Also, as I said as well, she is my lady-in-waiting which means she is always extremely respectful when she is not being strict which I think is silly. (I think lots of things about being a queen are silly but I must never say so and I do think it is nice to be able to do nice things for people that I could never do before.) I am much better friends with Esmel, who is Cavalia's daughter and my age. We play many things together which I am sure Cavalia would not like. Or Brida either, who is my other lady-in-waiting and she is much nicer than Cavalia but still she is quite strict.

Esmel is also my cousin Afiawyr's daughter (Cavalia is Afiawyr's wife) and Afiawyr as I am sure you know is ruling for me until I am fifteen. My parents did not want to rule. Did you know it happened that Berwyn and Eldrast were my mother and father all along? I was very excited to have a mother and father again as you will probably not be surprised to hear. They have been very sad but I read them your letter and they were very interested it seemed in the last part and lately Mother has been smiling more and Father plays with me much more than he used. They asked me that if I wrote you in return I should tell you it is not your fault that Einur died. It is not only they that think it is not your fault. I do not think it was. Although I miss him so much! You must not tell anyone because a queen should not do such a thing, but I cry a great deal when I am alone. Einur took care of me for a long time and certainly do not tell anyone this but although I love my real father very much I sometimes feel as though Einur is more like my father.

Did you know there was such excitement here just over a month ago! Actually it was the night after my birthday which is how I remember it was that long ago. Haledon captured Vaal, that nasty man who left me with Malia, very soon after you left (and do not worry about running away, I do not think you are a coward because it was truly awful and I would likely have run away myself if I could), along with another man named Glest who was also very nasty. They were hiding in the woods after our enemies departed. I got to sit on my throne wearing my crown and a very lovely dress and say "For crimes against my royal person and that of the late King Einur, I the Queen condemn you both to ten years in the dungeons of the Third Tribe." It was really very like being a Queen but I do not think I should like to do that again. I felt sorry for them and I think it is horrible to be shut up in the dark for ten years. Although the gaolers did let them out in the sunshine thrice a week. We are not cruel people, Afiawyr said.

But I must tell you of the excitement last month! I woke in the middle of the night to a great deal of shouting. You will not believe it but Vaal and Glest were attempting to make an escape! I regret to say that Glest was shot with an arrow as he ran and he sadly died at once. Vaal however succeeded in getting away and no one has seen him. Father thinks we shall probably never see him again. I hope not. I really am glad in the end that he got away, for I doubt he shall hurt anyone ever again now that the Illyrië are gone, and it is better to be living in the wild than shut up in a dungeon. Even

Glest is better off now if you ask me. Although Eigion, who is an old man who visits us every few months, says there is a horrid place where bad people go that is not with the Master so I hope Glest is not there.

I think I must close this letter. Cavalia is pestering me to prepare for a party we are going to with the sea fairies. As you know the Tribe now lives on the Island of Hornlë but we often visit the Sands of Lybroë because Afiawyr tells me for many, many years they all lived there with the sea fairies. Their King, Aldindir, always has me sit next him and he tells me such lovely stories about the fairies. He also has stories about Einur because Einur stayed with them for a while, but I shall have to tell you those stories in another letter because I really must go!

Come visit us, Gernhr. I miss you.

Twenty-second day, eighth month, twelfth year of the Freeing.

Just a quick note, Gernhr and Kania, to congratulate you on the birth of your *eleventh* child. Now you really must visit. You should be ashamed for putting it off so long. I have not seen you since Eihyr was two years old and I believe he was your fifth. Three sets of twins and they must drive you off your feet, not to mention the other five children, but dare I suggest you might manage the journey when baby Alanara is a few months old? After all you must see Klenora and tell me if she does not look *exactly* like Haledon. He claims she does not, that she is *my* double, but you must tell him he is wrong.

*E*ighth day of the sixth month of the thirteenth year of the Freeing.

We are safely home, although what possessed Haledon to present an eight-year-old boy with a dagger I shall never know – it's in despite of that dagger that we are safe home in the first place. Although Ardus was heartbroken when we did so, Kania and I had to put it away; he too nearly killed too many of Eadmod's sheep.

Lody, your little Klenora is an angel – she has your eyes and Haledon's... well, honestly I believe she looks much like you.

Do you remember years ago when I wrote you and told you that you were uppermost to Einur and that he died for you? He did it so you'd have a chance to grow up safe; I know because I would have done the same for my own little sister if Einur hadn't fixed for the Illyrië a whole year before her birth. I know he swore he'd be with you forever and you believe he can see you from wherever he is. I'm not so sure about the latter, but if he can I know he's smiling – with your little family, you're the most joyful girl I've ever met. Truly, Lody, he died for exactly that.

CONTINUE READING
FOR A PREVIEW

THE STARS GLEAM BRIGHTER

BY BENITA J. PRINS

1

IT WAS JUST DAWN. THE EARLY MORNING SUN SHONE brightly on the Malarn Lake. The rays pierced the shadows in every hollow of the surrounding meadows. A few clouds swam lazily through the deep blue sky.

Ringard looked up at the sun. It did not hurt his eyes – no light was too bright for the eyes of the Startern people. Ringard was a Startern; but though his home was in Staran with King Kanethon and his kin, he and his brother Pluriel had lived here in Fortaer for some years. Ringard was tall and slender, with dark eyes and hair that was blacker than black:

the typical Startern colouring.

Now as he looked a cloud passed over the sun, a grey cloud, dark grey. He shivered slightly. A few light drops of rain fell. With a worried look in his face he turned and entered the city.

Serpent's Road was a distasteful area of the city of Malarn, where pickpockets prowled the bustling marketplace and foreigners jabbered in strange tongues. Still, the Silver Spear Inn was well-kept and a pleasant enough place to eat dinner of an evening.

Ringard rang the bell on the counter, then turned around and surveyed the common room as he waited for Galdore to come. Most of the patrons of the Silver Spear were townsfolk, but today there were a few Gausher, from the land of Gaush across the mountains.

"What can we get for you today?"

Galdore, the twenty-three-year-old innkeeper, had taken over the running of the inn when his father had died a year ago. He was a generally gentle-spoken young man in keeping with his shoulder-length gold hair and dark blue eyes, but no one had tried to cheat him since a seedy stranger had attempted to do so five months earlier. Galdore had beaten the Gausher soundly; the vanquished thief had slunk off to one of the poorer taverns of Malarn.

"The usual, please, Galdore," Ringard replied.

"That would be baked chicken with a mug of ale? If you'll find yourself a seat, I'll send Tristal round directly."

"*Samach ne*," Ringard thanked Galdore as he made for an empty table in the far corner of the room.

As he waited for his food, Ringard listened to the rumours circulating the room. One working-class fellow was telling his friend about strange shadows he'd seen in the town square on his way home the previous night. Apparently these shadows had moved about the square with nothing to cast them. Another troublemaker informed anyone who would listen that the governor of the city of Forran, King Leftar's nephew Eparne, was conspiring to overthrow his uncle. Some of the ideas put forth were so ridiculous that Ringard was hard put not to laugh aloud.

A few minutes passed before Tristal arrived. He was Galdore's brother, two years younger, but could have been his twin as far as looks went. Tristal was carrying a platter loaded with fragrant chicken, potatoes, and beans, plus a quart of ale. Ringard dropped two copper pennies into the young man's hand.

"It smells delicious, as usual."

As Ringard ate his dinner, a cloaked figure slid into the seat across from him.

"Pluriel! There you are at last. I was beginning to wonder what had happened to you."

"Sorry I'm late, but I came as soon as I could. I overheard something as I came through the market after speaking with King Leftar. I believe it could be important."

Ringard swallowed his mouthful. "Go ahead, tell me."

"I expect you don't remember the prophecy of the Great Seer regarding the Sword of the Star?"

Ringard shook his head.

"'When the Star falls from the sky, the Sword of the Star shall be restored,'" Pluriel half-chanted. His brother looked up.

"You remember the tale about the theft of the Sword of the Star from the Golden Palace – how the minions of Jalavak broke in by night and took the ancient sword, secreting it in Duskmoor Keep."

"Yes, I recall that," Ringard said. "But what can the first part of the prophecy mean? 'When the Star falls from the sky.' It makes no sense. To which star does it refer? And how is it possible for a star to fall from the sky?"

"Royaleisia," muttered Pluriel, looking around to make sure no one was near enough to hear what he said. The room was beginning to empty out, however, and they enjoyed a little more privacy. A few dishes clattered as Tristal cleared a vacated table nearby.

Ringard paused for a moment before replying. Then he nodded slowly. "You believe the legends and peasants' tales?"

"Yes, I do." Pluriel shoved his chair back and stood up, looking down at his brother. "I am going to the Nevarra Swamp to make an attempt at recovering the Sword. You know it's the only weapon with which Jalavak can be defeated. Well, if we can get it back, then we have a chance of finally ending his reign over the South. Will you come with me, brother?"

"Of course I'll come with you!" Ringard exclaimed. "Do you think I'd let you face the dragon-keeper alone?"

Pluriel laughed, releasing some tension from his face. "I don't know that it's actually a *dragon* that guards the Sword, but I'll be glad of your company in any event."

As Pluriel reseated himself, two mugs of ale slid across the table and the other two chairs scraped back.

"How is your meal?" asked Galdore. "I trust you are not disappointed?"

Ringard shook his head. "It's very good, just as I expected."

"I'm glad," Galdore replied. "But Tristal says we may be able to give you more than just your supper."

"What do you mean?" Pluriel asked, looking suspiciously from Galdore to Tristal.

"In what would we need help?"

Galdore smiled. "No fear, we're friends of yours and foes of Jalavak's. My brother was telling me that you two were discussing the possibility of recovering the Sword of the Star."

"What is it to you?" questioned Pluriel.

"We wish to serve our King and help to end the tyranny of Jalavak. If you intend to go to Nevarra, we will go with you – if you permit it."

Ringard looked to Pluriel. "I would accept their offer, but this is your idea."

Pluriel turned a discerning stare on Galdore and Tristal. "What's your purpose in wanting to join us?"

Tristal shrugged. "Nothing more than what Galdore has told you." He flashed a brief smile. "Although I have always had a wish to do great things for Fortaer."

Settling back against the wall, Pluriel sat in silence for some time, his eyes closed. Finally he opened them and grinned. "I suppose it's all right. But," he continued, his smile disappearing, "you understand the danger. We may well not return."

The resolution on their faces did not waver.

"We are coming with you no matter what," Tristal stated.

Pluriel smiled again. "I'll speak with the King tomorrow. Any such expedition would have to be undertaken with his prior approval."

"It's an interesting idea," said the King, staring out the window, "but I'm not at all convinced it's a good one. First, it's based on conjecture. You are only assuming that this prophecy could be about to come true. And I hardly like to risk you and Ringard on a mere conjecture. The thing would be extremely risky. If the legends speak true, then the keeper of the Sword is a dragon, old and wily. That is assuming," he continued, turning around, "that you could reach the Nevarra Swamp safely in the first place. Jalavak has watchful eyes in all lands."

"I'm sure we could reach the Swamp easily enough. The main problem would be find the Sword, of course." Pluriel seemed about to go on, but King Leftar had turned back to the window and was no longer paying much attention.

A long and uncomfortable silence ensued, during which Pluriel stood awkwardly staring at the King's back. Finally the monarch looked round again and spoke one word.

"No."

Pluriel started. He hadn't been expecting Leftar to speak just then, and the terse dismissal of his request startled him further.

"No?" he questioned stupidly.

"No," repeated the King. "It's too dangerous. You and your brother are too helpful here for me to let you go on a suicide journey. I would be insane to do so."

He made a curt gesture with his hand, signalling that the audience was over. Pluriel opened his mouth one more time, but closed it with a sigh before any words came out. He backed out of the chamber, then strode down the hall, his angry footsteps fading away.

King Leftar tapped his empty goblet sharply on

the table. *Tap tap tap, tap TAP tap.* He couldn't get that stupid prophecy out of his mind. Stupid? All right, not stupid; prophets' words were inspired by Elamm'. It was the fact that Pluriel and his brother wanted to leave Fortaer that disturbed him.

You can't keep them forever, he reminded himself. Yet surely he had given Pluriel the right answer.

"Uncle?"

Not Eparne again. Not now. The King smiled tightly. "Come in, Eparne."

His nephew sauntered in. "Something the matter?"

Well, he didn't like Eparne, but he needed to talk this out with someone. "Pluriel Frosind-alon wants to go look for the Sword."

"Of the Star?"

"Exactly."

"And you said yes, of course?" Was that a slight gleam in Eparne's eye? No. Of course not. Eparne was nigh a brother to the Frosindalion.

"I said no," the King stated tersely, filling his goblet and taking a good sip.

"Why's that?" queried Eparne, pouring himself some wine uninvited.

Leftar laughed, humourlessly. "Perhaps because Ringard and Pluriel happen to be two of my best advisers?"

"Yeees..." drawled Eparne, drawing out the word. "But, you know, if they could get the Sword for you, you would possess the immediate advantage over Jalavak. An advantage, forgive me, which I think you sorely need."

Leftar looked up and thought for a moment. "I could send someone to the Swamp, I suppose," he said hesitantly. "Perhaps – "

"You can't send just anyone, uncle," Eparne cut in. "It has to be someone you can trust. If I were you, I would choose the Frosindalion. Ringard and Pluriel are your best chance."

The King hesitated for a time. Then he shook his head.

Eparne continued to make his case. *Can the boy never leave others' affairs alone?* "They could make the trip in three months or less," he pushed.

"They could also be killed in the doing of it," Leftar pointed out testily.

"Oh, it's a slight possibility, but very unlikely, you know. Pluriel is one of Fortaer's foremost swordsmen, and Ringard is not far behind in prowess." *Isn't that the precise reason I'm reluctant to let them go?* "I think it would be quite safe if they were to find a few friends to go with them."

He stared at the King. Leftar thought carefully for some time, weighing in his mind all possible outcomes of his decision either way. Finally he nodded.

"Summon Pluriel back."

AVAILABLE NOW

ABOUT THE AUTHOR

Benita J. Prins has been writing since she was six years old. Her imagination likes to work over time, and this is at the root of her love for fantasy. She loves to be inventing and feels at a loss when she doesn't have a fantasy location to flesh out.

When not writing, Benita keeps busy with music, graphic design, and increasing her already enormous book collection. Some of her favourite authors are J.R.R. Tolkien, C.S. Lewis, Melanie Dickerson, John Buchan, and Jane Austen. Benita lives in Ontario, Canada.

BY THE SAME AUTHOR

The Stars Gleam Brighter
(previously published as *Starscape*)

Aratar, Peredhil, and Halflings, Oh My!:
The Ultimate Tolkien Quiz